THE MONOCHROME SOLUTION

DAVID L. LITVIN

THE MONOCHROME SOLUTION

David L. Litvin

Cover Design by A Novel Idea Author Services.

2nd Edition

Published in the United States of America by:

David L. Latvin

www.davidlitvin.com

For Skye, Louis, Assata, Kendra and Brian
For all the people still trying to fix it
For Linda Cirruto, still the best person I know
And Susan, who hopefully made some sense of this.

PROLOGUE

My hometown of Allset, New York, has almost always been anything but. True story: the town got its name as part of a failed and embarrassing attempt to insult Thomas Edison.

By 1885 it was already publicly known that Edison would be building a gigantic new laboratory, having outgrown the already legendary location in Menlo Park, New Jersey. Armed with this knowledge and dangerous with misplaced confidence, city elders hatched a plan to lure Edison to tour the town. Surely the great man would fall prey to the charms of what was then called Hope Springs. The town was called Hope Springs despite the lack of any actual springs or any apparent reason for hope.

Nevertheless, they were successful in that Edison did indeed tour the town, that is to say if a single ride down Main Street in a horse-drawn carriage counts as a "tour." There is no evidence that Edison ever seriously considered Hope Springs for his new laboratory. There aren't even any documents that prove he ever answered the elders' repeated inquiries. Basically they had been rebuffed, ignored. And there would not be an Edison laboratory in Hope Springs.

It is fair to say that the town didn't take rejection well. In 1890 the town council voted unanimously to change the name of the town to Allset. "Why Allset?" you may ask. Good question. You see, by that time, it was well known that Nicola Tesla was a bitter rival of Edison's. What better way to disrespect Edison than to name the town in honor of the anti-Edison? They were being clever by spelling it backwards. They were daft for spelling it wrong with an extra *l,* which no one discovered until it was too late. At that point, they just stuck with it. It would be less embarrassing than to change the name again.

So Allset it would remain. And for a time, the name seemed appropriate. The town had better luck with Monsanto. They opened a sprawling factory in the town in 1895. It became the economic engine of Allset and lured other companies and factories to the town by the early 20th century. At its peak, the Monsanto plant employed more than 1,400 people. By 1920 the town had a population of over 8,000, by 1950 over 13,000. The town had weathered the Great Depression with barely a blip. In fact, the town gained population during the early 1930s. It was one of the few bright spots on the East Coast where the desperate might be able to find work. The two world wars were no problem. The factories were converted to making munitions, and Allset had remained relatively prosperous throughout.

In 1968 Monsanto announced that the now ancient plant would shut down permanently by 1970. Other companies followed suit, and by 1975 there was virtually no manufacturing in the town of Allset. The town survived as a remote and inexpensive suburb of the relatively prosperous Albany, Schenectady, and Troy. Many of the older engineers, factory workers, and machinists stayed for their retirement, but their children were leaving in bunches, and by 1990 the population had dropped to about 5,000 and was still declining.

All hope for the former Hope Springs looked lost, but in 1993 it once again found its luck. Monsanto had leased the property that was home to their factory. As it turns out, the land actually belonged to the Nonya band of Native Americans of New York State. There weren't a whole lot of them, and none of them lived anywhere near Allset, but a sharp group of New York City investment lawyers had figured out a way to build a casino on what was legally tribal land. It would be the Nonya's casino, but the lawyers would take care of the regulatory and financing issues in exchange for a hefty cut. Allset would be home to only the second casino in all of New York State and the fifth largest in the country outside of Nevada. Not too shabby.

The casino itself was also not too shabby. It had a massive slot floor, plenty of table games, and a fifty-table poker room, this being just as poker was beginning to be televised and popular. It had a buffet, a diner, and two upscale restaurants to keep the gamblers well fed and gambling. They didn't go too crazy on the hotel. Consultants had told them that Allset would mostly be a day trip destination, so the investors put most of their money into the casino. But they did build a well-appointed, 250-room hotel for those who wished to stay. They called it The Hope Springs Casino at Allset in honor of the town's original name of Hope Springs. Everyone I know just calls it Hope or The Hope—or on a bad day gambling, Hopeless.

For both the Nonyas and the town, it was an instant hit. The casino created hundreds of jobs, and those new workers needed to live somewhere. Housing prices in Allset nearly doubled overnight, and there was a mini boom of new housing construction. It also created hundreds of well-paying casino jobs. During its first five years of operation, it was consistently among the twenty most profitable casinos in the world. We still never saw a whole lot of the Nonya tribal members, but it's a safe bet they were pretty happy with the way things were going. The tribe had less than 1,200 members, which amounted to a pretty hefty take for each member of the tribe. I'm sure that after a couple of years, each and every one of them could afford a house in the Hamptons if that was what they wanted. What they didn't want, apparently, was to be around the casino—or the town of Allset.

As usual with Allset, the good times didn't last. Other tribes in New York had learned the same trick, and new tribal casinos were popping up all over the place. Soon there were even slot machines in New York City. Eventually the competition took its toll on the Nonya's casino and chipped away at its popularity and profits. The Nonyas had always been good stewards of the property, and for more than a decade had reinvested to always keep it looking fresh and new. But as revenues declined, so did the investment, and eventually the casino became a bit threadbare and rundown. It just didn't make sense to pump money into the place as revenues settled in at about a fifth of what they had been at their peak.

Around this same time, the Nonyas found a new tenant for what was the site of the old Monsanto plant, which was nearby but out of sight from the casino property. GeneWorks was a very well capitalized, privately held biotech startup. Its ownership was a bit mysterious, but its funding certainly wasn't. They prepaid in its entirety a twenty-five year lease on the property with the Nonyas, then completely razed the remains of the old Monsanto plant and built a massive, state-of-the-art laboratory in its place. It had taken more than a hundred years, but Allset finally had its high-tech, scientifically cutting-edge laboratory.

GeneWorks had hit Allset with a massive PR blitz, touting hundreds of construction jobs to later be replaced with perhaps thousands more permanent jobs. The town, of course, had been more than sufficiently wooed. They happily offered tax breaks, built a new network of roads around the plant, and had the obligatory groundbreaking ceremony with the mayor and city council members holding shovels and smiling wide for the cameras. No members of the Nonya Tribe attended the ceremony. The finished, gleaming laboratory was opened to great civic pride and fanfare less than two years later, about a year before I made my own return to Allset.

As for the casino, I don't think it will ever go out of business, but it became the place near the highway that you stopped by on your way to someplace else. Maybe that's what Allset has always been, the place you stopped by on your way to someplace else. Just like Edison did.

1

A MAN AND HIS DRINKING BUDDY

My name is Ray Louis, a combination of my father's two favorite fighters, Sugar Ray Robinson and Joe Louis. My father is Brian Louis and was a single father long before it was fashionable. My mother died of a ruptured brain aneurysm four days after giving birth to me, their only child. He never spoke much about her, but it is safe to say that she was the only woman my father ever loved, not that there weren't others later on.

Growing up, I didn't know or think too much about it, but looking back, he would occasionally introduce me to women that he called "friends." Even then, I knew that they weren't like his other friends or drinking buddies. I knew that because I was one of his drinking buddies, not that he gave me booze when I was a kid, but for as long as I could remember, I was one of his group of friends—his best friend, to be sure.

These days, the shrinks would probably say it is an unhealthy way to raise a child, but it has always worked for us. I never felt cheated, and my dad was *always* there for me. My guess is that after my mom died, he needed a friend a lot more than he needed a son, and like I said, it was never a problem for us.

It's not a utopian relationship to be sure. We are both a little too smart for our own good. We are both right so often that we don't have much practice in being wrong even when we are wrong. But we were, are, and always will be best friends and drinking buddies.

Brian Louis was, until his recent retirement, a mathematician, an actuary, and semi-professional poker player. The only reason I wouldn't call him a professional is that poker was never his primary source of income. He was always a consistently profitable player but never chose to rely on poker for our income. When asked, he would always say, "No one ever wins when they *have* to win." Poker becomes a much harder game when you need to win to pay the bills.

For years he traveled regularly for consulting work. Once I was old enough to walk, he would bring me along for days or sometimes weeks at a time. He would keep me out of school, but when we got back, I would always find a way to catch up. On the road, my father would always find time to show me around whatever city we were in. I wish I had appreciated it more at the time. Before I had turned sixteen, I had traveled to almost every big city in the U.S. and a few in Europe, Japan, and China. It's not a coincidence that we would regularly find ourselves in Las Vegas. In Vegas my dad's relatives would sometimes watch me when my father was working or playing. My aunts and uncles took me to Lake Mead, the Grand Canyon, and Mount Charleston. It all seemed normal to me and, of course, I didn't appreciate it then as much as I would now.

As my father aged and computers took over he had less need to travel and was able to do most of his work from our home in *Allset*. The only downside was the crazy hours. He was paid well but he usually had to be awake and available for clients in time zones around the world, so day and night meant something different in our house than it did in most.

We are both night owls. I am not sure if we both were born that way or it was that we had to adapt to the crazy hours we kept. But it always worked for us. Of course, we are alike in other ways too. We share a gift. I would call it math skills, but it's not exactly that. It's more about basic math, percentages, and probabilities combined with practical application. It is also an ability to identify patterns, themes, and make instant accurate assessments. I guess the best way to describe it would be "thinking on your feet." My father would jokingly call it "the Force." Don't get me wrong. He is no genius; we're not talking Einstein here. There are no grand theories or vast knowledge, but there is efficient gathering and use of the knowledge at hand.

Confused? Me too. It's tough to describe but easy for us to see. We notice it instantly when we meet anyone else with similar skills.

Poker always seemed to be the ideal game for people with our abilities, and I have been playing the game for as long as I can remember. Of course, I couldn't go into the casino as a child, but one of my earliest memories was playing poker with my father and his friends. I think I was three. We were in our house, sitting around a nine-foot regulation poker table that we still have to this day. It has a real poker table rail and felt cloth. We also had an oval wood insert that turned it into an almost proper dining room table, but it didn't get used for that very often.

On my 18th birthday, it was time to "Head for The Hope," to quote from one of the casino's earliest advertising slogans. Entering the poker room for the first time was like a homecoming. There were about a hundred people playing, spread out across thirteen active tables. I think I already knew about half of those people, many of whom had passed through our dining room at one time or another.

By this time, The Hope poker room was already well past its glory days. It was still a huge fifty-table room, but more than half of those tables never saw any action. On any given weekday, the room would peak at about fifteen active tables, all of which were clustered together in the part of the room nearest the three most important things to a poker player: the bar, the snack bar, and the toilets. The cashier's cage was just outside the poker room on the main slot floor. At eighteen I could not go in there since the minimum age for slot play was twenty-one, whereas poker was eighteen. It didn't matter much since chips could be bought at the table. A pit boss would always cash out my winnings.

The Hope was already past its prime, but it was still a pretty nice poker room even by national standards. It had high ceilings with massive crystal chandeliers. It was a bit dated but still beautiful and mostly kept clean. The carpet, like the table felts, was a pale blue meant to suggest the color of a spring but still had the overly busy design elements that casinos use to keep the floors from looking dirty and worn. By this time they did look worn, but they were thickly padded, which still conveyed a sense of opulence. It also helped to reduce the constant noise of clattering chips and complaining players.

For the next two years, my dad and I were a nearly daily presence. We gently milked the room and its recreational players for a few hundred dollars a week. We used "the Force" as my father would say, and it wasn't long before I built up a decent bankroll for college. Brian Louis did not insist on much, but he did insist that I go to college, saying, "Life is like poker. You gotta read the books. Even if you never use the knowledge, you at least have to know what they know. And then you can know more."

2

THE NOT SO PRODIGAL SON

If my father was disappointed that I went to college in Las Vegas, he certainly never showed it. I knew he was going to miss me, and I sure as hell was going to miss him. We had been companions since the day I was born, but we both knew the casino business was a natural for me, and there was no better place to get that education than UNLV. I enrolled in their Gaming Management program.

Money was not a big problem. My father paid for everything school related. That meant books, classes, and fees. I was expected to pay living expenses. I had built up a decent bankroll, and it didn't take me long to find the right places to play in Vegas. At first it was a little harder to grind out a living in Vegas than it was back home. After a while I found the right games. That meant looking in the higher end strip casinos but not too high end. I learned the hard way a couple of times when I strayed into games that were too big for my bankroll.

Somewhere along the way, a guy named Chris Moneymaker lucked into a million-dollar payday in the World Series of Poker, and all of a sudden, No-Limit Texas Hold'em was the hottest poker game in town. In limit poker, the bets on each card are set in advance. In no limit poker, you can bet all the chips in front of you at any time.

That may sound like heaven for me and my father, but it's actually a giant pain in the ass. It has to do with variables. In limit poker, you simply play the odds and observe your opponents' tendencies. It's pretty straightforward, and a bad luck card or two can't make or break your day. I am pretty sure I can win playing limit Texas Hold'em while having an appendectomy. In No Limit Hold'em, a single bad card can ruin your week. A short period of "running bad" can destroy your bankroll. Yes, you can win more playing well, but the swings can be massive.

My father always said that No Limit poker became popular because it allowed amateurs like Moneymaker to compete against professionals because luck was such a big factor. It made poker more like a slot machine than a game of skill. I agree, but a skilled player still has an edge in No Limit. You just have to be willing to tolerate bigger swings and more drastic peaks and valleys.

And it made the most important factor even more important: finding the right game. To put it bluntly, that means you want to find the most clueless opponents possible. My father's favorite saying was one I heard about a thousand times growing up: "I don't mind being the tenth worst poker player on earth as long as I get to play with the nine who are even worse than me." To be a winning player you must always find the best games with the worst players.

I was able to nurse my bankroll through the ups and downs and kept my wits about me long enough to earn a Bachelor's Degree in Gaming Management from UNLV. Like my father, I knew I didn't want to depend on playing poker as my main source of income. I quickly got a job at one of the big resort casinos on the strip.

It was a management training program, and it didn't pay that much at first, but it was the start of my real education in the industry. The catch was that I had to sign on for at least four years. The first six months were a crash course in learning to deal every casino game. I learned to deal dice, blackjack, roulette, and almost all of the newer games that we called "carnival games." Carnival games like Casino War and others were a novelty and carried a huge edge for the house. Ironically, the only game they didn't teach me to deal was poker, which operated as a separate entity from the casino games, much like Keno and the sports book were considered different departments. Poker dealer training is something I could get by without. I was dealing cards to my father and his friends since I was old enough to hold a deck. With my formal training in other casino games, it's a safe bet that I could easily handle dealing poker in a casino if the need ever arose, which to the best of my recollection it never did.

The next eighteen months were even more exciting and challenging. Well, most of it was exciting. I spent about two months at a time in different departments of the resort: two months in table games, two months in slots, followed by stints in keno, surveillance, security, and then finally, some time in the poker room. I suppose I could have gotten out of it, but I even spent two months cleaning guest rooms and sweeping up trash as part of the housekeeping staff.

In all, it was eighteen months of first-hand learning about every part of a massive resort casino and hotel. My favorite part? Dealing craps. At six foot one, I am a little tall for a dice dealer. The best are about five foot ten, which is tall enough to reach everything but not so tall as to be constantly crouched over. But despite the backache, I really loved dealing the game. At a busy table, the game was electric, and you could feed off the energy. Time flew. The irony is that I have never played dice. Not once. Nor have I ever played a slot machine, a keno ticket, or the lottery. To my father these were games for suckers. What point was there to playing a game you could never win? In my family it would be a bigger sin to play a slot machine than to shoot up heroin. Both were dangerous and expensive.

After this internship I settled in as an assistant casino shift manager on a graveyard shift that included weekends. Of course, I didn't mind the hours, but graveyard always had an odd rhythm. Our graveyard shift was 10 p.m. to 6:30 a.m., so on a Saturday night, I would come into a packed casino moving at warp speed, and then by 3 a.m. it would be desolate. The few remaining guests would mostly be drunk or stuck or both, chasing their losses or highs from the night before.

Our casino was also popular with the "in the biz" crowd from other casinos. Dealers, bartenders, and some of the show people liked our place as a late night hangout. Even for me it was a little weird leaving work as the sun rose but not so weird that I went home. A pretty steady group of my fellow graveyard shift workers would head to a joint downtown for breakfast, drinks, gambling, or all of the above.

I would drink, but I almost never got drunk. I would gamble just to kill time and fit in but only on the few remaining video poker machines that offered a tiny player edge with perfect play. Like my father, I have the gift of moderation. And it really is a gift. I think it's genetics . . . or luck. In my father's family, there has not been a single drug addict, alcoholic, or compulsive gambler as far back as anyone can remember. When I was growing up, I used to think that was true of everyone. When I got to Vegas, I learned quickly that the true normal was that virtually every family but mine was plagued by addiction in one form or another.

Sometimes I amuse myself by thinking of a comic book superhero that I would call "Moderation Man." He would have a modest cape, and he could eat just one cookie. Okay, so it's not a superpower, but I bet if you ask any addict, it is a power that they would be happy to have.

It was in downtown Vegas in the early morning hours that I met Shirley, my first and so far only love. As a gambling man, I would be willing to bet that if your name were Shirley, you would change it or call yourself something else—which is exactly what Shirley did. She just called herself Lee. We were already dating about a year and living together before I found out about this Shirley person. Such was her lack of enthusiasm for her first name. It was the mail she received at our apartment that gave her away.

Lee was a bartender at a casino downtown where I would hang out at after work. She was everything that I thought I liked at the time. She was funny and quick-witted in the way that a good, friendly bartender can be. And she was beautiful, tall and blonde like the cliché southern California girl that she was. Born and raised in LA, she had come to Vegas to be a dancer. She was classically trained and had no problem finding gigs in Las Vegas until a series of injuries took their toll and ended her dancing career. I hadn't thought about it before, but I learned that injuries in professional dancing were as common and career ending as they were in many athletes.

If Lee had any lingering despair at going from featured dancer to late night bartender, I certainly never saw it. She was always positive and pragmatic. She also knew that just like dancing, she couldn't bartend forever, so she was at UNLV slowly working on a degree in physical therapy, already planning the career that would one day replace bartending.

I really thought she was out of my league, and it took me several weeks, and then several beers, to work up the nerve to ask her to breakfast one morning. It's not that I think I am ugly. Lee actually described me as a poor man's Ben Affleck. She meant that as a compliment. It's certainly not a compliment to

Ben Affleck. To my surprise, she said yes. I think we were both surprised at how compatible we were and how quickly we became comfortable with each other. I don't mean comfortable in the taking-each-other-for-granted way but more like our time with each other immediately felt natural and relaxed.

As good as our relationship was, I think we both knew it was not meant to be forever, just like I knew that I didn't intend to live in Vegas permanently. At 30 years old, I had been living in Las Vegas for almost a decade, the last five years of it with Lee. When I told her I was moving back to New York, I invited her to come with me, and I meant it. But I also knew she wouldn't come. Almost her whole family now lived in Vegas, and she wanted to have kids, something she knew I did not want. I believe to this day that we really do love each other. The truth is, I probably would have married her and had kids with her just to make her happy. Thank goodness that one of us (her!) was grown-up enough to keep us from doing that to each other.

By that point, I was director of gaming at a local casino several miles from the strip. I gave four weeks' notice at my job. I left Lee everything in our apartment and pre-paid the rent for six months, which was the rest of our current lease. She could have probably afforded it on her own, but I wanted her to have options. And just like that, I was headed east with nothing more than a car full of clothes.

I had never intended to spend my whole life in Vegas. For that matter, I don't intend to stay in New York forever either. The time just seemed right to spend a couple of years back home. With my resume, I could find a job at virtually any casino in the country, but I had not even begun to think about what might come next. For the moment, I could afford to just grind out a few bucks playing poker at The Hope, hang out with my dad, and see what might come next.

In his own way, my father was the reason I came back. At 72 (Yes, he was almost 42 when I was born), he was still in pretty good shape, but he and his buddies had hatched their plan. Twenty-five years ago, they had all agreed to buy long-term care insurance policies. The policies were designed to pay them $7,500 monthly income in the event that they required a nursing home or assisted living. My dad and his four friends were now all in their early seventies. Funny thing: the medical papers they needed to qualify for their policies to pay off were all filled out by the same doctor in the same week. Even funnier: as a strange coincidence, they all qualified just after the assisted living facility found itself with five apartments available right near each other.

The place was called Springview. Of course, there was not any actual spring in sight, but it was a really nice place nonetheless. My father and his friends would each have a fully paid-off apartment in a beautiful building that provided everything, including meals. They would be living in their very own, fully paid for codger gambling camp. Even better, when they did eventually need help, they would have it.

I had heard him and his friends talk about this plan for years, but I was still impressed with the ruthless efficiency with which they had pulled it off. My father and I had talked for the last year about my returning to Allset.

A month before he moved, he called me and said, and I quote, "Okay, Ray, it's time to shit or get off the pot. Either come take the house, or I am going to sell the fuckin' thing."

I asked, "What do you want me to do with it?"

"Well, for one thing, you can pay the taxes, insurance, and upkeep" and added, "Oh yeah, and you can shovel the fuckin' snow because I sure as shit don't want to do it anymore. But seriously, Ray, I want you to live in it. I want to keep it in the family. We have a lot of great memories in that house."

He was uncharacteristically warm and emotional when he

said that, but if there is one person I know, it is Brian Louis, so I was expecting what came next.

"And maybe I won't like the old folks' home. When I move back to the house, you can be there to change my shitty diapers."

That was more like it.

3

LITTLE ORPHAN ANNIE

My name is Ann Byron, and I now live in Allset, New York. How that came about is not all that unusual. I am a research scientist, and that is all I ever wanted to be since my grandma died when I was twelve years old. That was way more than two decades ago. She was still a young woman, not yet even fifty-five when she died of a disease so rare, it barely had a name and definitely no cure. As rare as it was, it was even rarer among Black women. She was the first Black woman to die of this disease in more than thirty years. From that day forward, I knew exactly what I wanted to do. In my twelve-year-old brain, I was going to manage my grief by making it my business to stop twelve-year-old girls from losing their grandmas to disease.

I know lots of people feel that way with the loss of a loved one, but with me it stuck. It simply never went away. I was going to systematically find a way to cure every disease that took away grandmas.

This ambition motivated me to excel in school, where up to that point, I had basically just screwed around and gotten by. It led me to Northwestern University where I earned two bachelor's and one master's degree and finally, after years of work, earned a doctorate in clinical technology. As you might expect, I was heavily recruited out of university and spent most of the last two decades working in biotech research. My first job was as an assistant research associate, which was little more than a glorified lab tech. I'm not complaining, but at that time, biotech was still an industry dominated by white men. While there was no overt sexism, overt racism, or overt harassment—nobody ever told me to get their coffee or chased me around a desk—it was still seven or eight men for every woman at my level. And I was the only Black woman.

This rarity was no evil plot. It was the result of history. More and more women and people of color were entering the science fields, but it was a slow process. It was the result of centuries of sexism, racism, and cultural norms that presumed women were not cut out for this sort of thing. I was always grateful that it was never that hard for me, but these kinds of things take time. I am still ridiculously dedicated, generally competent, and situationally creative, traits that have advanced my career in a way that any lingering sexism or racism could not hinder.

You could argue that my nickname is the result of a bit of sexism, but I would not. "Little Orphan Annie" is the name I earned early on in my career and has stuck with me to this day. I like it. It makes sense. Of course, my name is Ann, and I have spent my life trying to find cures for rare diseases, the type often called "orphans" in the pharmaceutical industry. The diseases are so rare, there cannot possibly be profit in finding the cure for a disease that affects so few people. Research and development costs are just too high and the potential earnings just too low, so there is no profit, and therefore no incentive, to find a cure for diseases like the one that killed my grandma. They are the orphans of the medical world, and I am "Little Orphan Annie."

Of course, there is *some* research into these diseases, and that has been the focus of my career. Funding will come, although not often enough, in the form of government or charitable grants to those often working in a university setting. Pharmaceutical giants will become involved later in the process with government or charitable assistance but sometimes not, depending on the potential market value of the eventual treatment or cure.

The lure that had brought me to Allset and GeneWorks (which I had barely heard of at the time) was irresistible. They were offering me an absurd amount of money and even more than that, almost complete control over the research, the budget, and the eventual published result. In essence, it was simply an offer I couldn't refuse.

The laboratory in Allset was to be something almost completely new. By all accounts, the company was fabulously and securely capitalized, a fact their representatives underscored to me and a few of my colleagues with a slickly produced PowerPoint and multimedia presentation. GeneWorks had used a similar presentation and a considerable lobbying effort to woo the U.S. Department of Defense into a massive and super-secret research project contract. The revenues from the military work would help to defray the costs of the orphan work that I would be leading. And I was proud. I would be the first woman, Black or white, to lead such an effort.

The laboratory itself was really two separate entities entirely, almost as if two separate buildings were placed back to back, sharing a common rear wall. The entrances to each were placed at opposite ends. My side would have no access to the other side and vice versa. Well, not quite *no* access. There was a single doorway connecting the two sides as an emergency exit, which was required by local fire code. Our side was unsecured. Presumably there would be guards or electronic monitoring or both on their side. The plants were identical in size, but that's where the similarities ended. My side would have the normal security of a modern laboratory, that is to say, there was *some* security. Nothing we would be working with was particularly secret or hazardous. The other side was extremely well secured, more so than even the most secure facilities I had seen in the past. I didn't give it much thought at the time. After all, it was a new town and a new facility.

I didn't have much trouble getting settled in Allset. It was a friendly enough town with everything your average, single, female scientist could need and one thing I would want—a casino.

Hope Springs casino was aging and a bit homely, but it had a big, comfortable poker room with good action, and that was all I ever looked for in a casino. I had been playing poker since I was a child, and it always suited my personality. Maybe it was just another white, male-dominated arena that I wanted to make my mark in. I will leave that for psychologists to decide.

I'm no poker pro, but I hold my own. If I took the time to add up all of my wins and losses over the years, I'm probably slightly to the plus side, which is better than most. And as for being single, I've had a few relationships over the years, but in the end, it always came back to the same thing: I would rather be by myself than with someone who sucks. I'm thinking that someday, someone will come along who doesn't suck. I don't mind waiting.

And that brings me to Ray Louis. He certainly does not suck either as a person or especially as a poker player. I had dated one white man some years back, and I felt no awkwardness or social pressure. He just wasn't the right man, Black or white. Anyway, when it comes to Ray, I make it my business in poker to keep an eye out for tough players, and he certainly fits the bill. He is mostly quiet at the table and extremely observant of the action and players even if he is not involved in the hand. He is clearly a pro or at the pro level.

Normally, I stay clear of players like that, but I found myself attracted to him both as a poker player and a man. He had a mostly quiet demeanor, but when he did speak, it was with a subtle intelligence and humor. To be honest, even as a cold, calculating poker player and scientist, I found it sexy. And he wasn't hard to look at. You might even call him a poor man's Mel Gibson—though I'm not sure Mel would find that to be a compliment.

The first time we actually spoke, there wasn't an immediate romantic spark. I was eating dinner in the diner at The Hope (which isn't too bad by the way), and I was surprised when he asked if he could join me. He had barely looked at me at the tables and certainly had never spoken to me.

He introduced himself, and I invited him to join me. He quickly launched into an explanation that his name was an homage to his dad's two favorite fighters. I'm no fan of boxing or mixed martial arts. I always thought it was homoerotic in the sense that it allowed otherwise macho men with homosexual tendencies to climb all over each other and touch each other's butts. Not that I mind. I appreciate a fit male body as much as the next girl, and I have no problem with anybody's sexuality. Just do whatever makes you happy. Love who you want. But I also can't help but think that these fighters might be happier finding a safer way to express those feelings, but hey, to each their own.

Ray was precise and deliberate. I soon learned that he had spent most of his life in the casino business. I also learned that he had returned to Allset to take care of his dad's house and his still vital and mischievous father who had somehow finagled his way into a luxurious assisted living facility along with his friends where they conducted their own private poker games in his apartment.

I had actually heard of the game. Players at The Hope often talked about being invited to or actually playing in "the codger game" not too far from the casino. I have to admit to being a bit miffed about never having been invited. Here I am a not bad looking, respectable poker player, and I had been excluded! I just chalked it up to lingering sexism or racism, that they were literally an "old boys' club" and left it at that. No girls allowed—especially no Black girls.

But the real answer was surprising and actually complimentary in a way. Ray explained that they had no interest in me for their game specifically *because* I am a good player. The group sent Ray, who did it reluctantly and carefully, to recruit only the most clueless of opponents, known in the poker world as "fish," who could then be promptly and completely skinned at the hands of the harmless-looking but crafty codgers down at the old folks home

Ray and I would become an interesting couple of sorts. We were obviously from vastly different backgrounds, but we shared a certain outlook and demeanor that we liked about each other. Neither of us had any real desire to date anyone else, and he was the only man I have ever had in my life who didn't object to my very demanding work schedule., nor did he seem threatened by my intelligence, occasional sarcasm, or almost slave-like devotion to my work. It was a nice fit, and I was perfectly comfortable seeing where it might lead.

For the moment, where it was leading was to takeout dinners at his place that usually lead to way better than average sex and the occasional sleepover, mostly on weekends. I admit to one slightly ulterior motive, an invite to the codger game at Springview. I knew it would be tough competition and more than likely a losing proposition, but I wanted to test my skills against real players and maybe learn a thing or two about a thing or two.

And I did. It didn't cost me too much either. In four trips into the old-person shark tank, I was stuck less than two hundred dollars, and I learned a lot. The biggest thing I learned is that to really play poker well, it is boring as fuck. Ray's dad described it as “two hours of boredom punctuated by two minutes of terror.”

And he was right, like he is about most things as far as I can tell. Playing in that game is fun. The men were funny and welcoming even after they realized that I wasn’t going to be a particularly profitable guest for them. It’s nice to know I am welcome, but it’s not like I have a lot of free time, so I mostly still play at The Hope where I am more like the shark and less like the fish.

4

BRIAN AND HIS RACIST POKER POSSE

I had never thought of myself as racist until I moved into this assisted living facility. I lived most of my life in Allset, a town populated by less than ten percent of Blacks, who to me were always very well behaved. My guess is that when you are a minority, being well behaved is a survival mechanism. The town itself had no real history of racial strife, and as far as I could tell, the small Black population suffered no overt racism —racism that up until recently I would have convinced myself I would never tolerate. I would tell my son, "Hate everybody equally," which was a joke but with a point. Everyone deserves a chance until they personally show you they don't.

My business has taken me all over the world, and if you had asked me six months ago, I would have told you that I am prejudiced against no one. I find the whole concept of racism disgusting—with the exception of prejudice against left-handed people and those who wear bow ties; they are not to be trusted. That was a joke, but this isn't.

When I moved into this facility, for the first time in my life, I found myself surrounded by Black people—not the residents; all but one is white. But the staff is ninety percent

Black, and among those, probably sixty percent are Jamaican. As a group, they speak with a delightful lilt. Unfortunately for them, they must occasionally tell me what to do, which is not something I've ever been keen on. And I came to a terrible discovery: I am racist in ways that I had never realized before—or had reason to. The very first time that a Black dining room attendant told me that I had come down too late to dinner and that the dining room was closed, I found myself with the following thought flashing across my consciousness: *Who the fuck is this Black motherfucker, and who the hell is she to tell me that I can't eat when I damn well please?*

That was the moment I realized it, so I punched her square in the jaw and sat down and ate my dinner like a person. No, I didn't. I actually cursed silently to myself and ordered a pizza delivered to my apartment, and as I ate, I started to earnestly reflect upon where that instinct had come from. I'm no Mother Theresa, but I have always tried to live my life by four simple words: "Don't be a dick." And racism of any kind is most definitely dickishness of the highest order.

So where did this come from? I'm old enough to remember the early days of the civil rights movement, and I was definitely a cheerleader, albeit from the sidelines. The night Obama was elected, I cried tears of joy—and I'm not a crier. It's not that I have anything against crying; I just don't generally do it. It's something I do pretty much only at funerals or if I happen to overhear country music.

My point is that I would never have thought of myself as racist, yet here I was confronting my own wildly dickish thoughts on the matter. Introspection is not my favorite pastime, nor am I particularly good at it, but this certainly seemed worth the time. Time was something I now had plenty of, and I didn't like what I discovered. I am racist—not in the overtly Donald Trump or David Duke kind of way but more in the "I wonder if that Black kid in Safeway is going to shoplift something" kind of way.

The sad part is, I don't know how to fix this. It's so basic and instinctual to hate "others" for anything you fear or don't like or anything that goes wrong, and Black people will always be the single most distinguishable "other." Sure, many groups have suffered discrimination all over the world forever, but when push comes to shove, you can change your name, change your religion, or learn a language to protect yourself from discrimination, at least to some extent. But unless your name is Michael Jackson, if you are Black, you will always be Black. It didn't even work out so well for him.

I've seen and heard more than my share of casual and overt racism over the years even from people I would otherwise consider nice. My friend Lenny, as nice a man as you'd ever want to meet, refers to the staff here collectively as "the shvatzas." That's the Yiddish word for Black people. I'm told it's nowhere near as bad as the n-word, but it certainly is not a compliment. Lenny is a Jew, and at seventy-two has encountered plenty of anti-Semitism. If someone like Lenny can reconcile in his head showing disrespect to Black people, who in the world could possibly be completely free of it? That led me to another answer I didn't much care for—NO ONE.

I once read a saying, and now I take credit for thinking of it. "We are the children of children, and we think as we are told." It is true. We are stuffed with every conceivable bias straight from the cradle, often without even realizing it. But that doesn't mean we need to be a slave to it. Like everything else worth doing in life, learning is a process and, as much as possible, a conscious choice. Keep the things of value that have been imprinted on us, and cast away the slime . . . like racism.

So that's what I am going to do. Even at my relatively advanced age, we have a responsibility to at least try to grow and learn. Lenny is not mean-spirited when he calls them "shvatzas," but it's wrong, and he should know better, especially given the horrors that his own people have suffered.

Not that they need my validation, but the Jamaican staff here are some of the most clever, hardworking, and resourceful people I have ever known. My four friends and I don't need much help with day-to-day activities just yet, but plenty of people here do. How would you like to walk ninety-year-olds to the bathroom all day? How would you like to wipe their nasty old asses? They do things like that all day, every day. In my mind, they are heroes. Whatever they are paid is not enough.

And all of this has led me down another rabbit hole. There were close to a hundred people of color working at Springview. None of them lived in Allset. Before moving in here, I had never met a single one of them. That means none of them live in Allset proper. So where are they coming from? I'm not going to bore you with the details. They all lived in predominantly Black neighborhoods slightly to the north of Allset.

I was trying to figure out how that works and why it happens, that even today, we have racial segregation. The answer was surprisingly simple: the U.S. government formally created, reinforced, and promoted separation of the races, mostly through Federal Housing Administration policy going back to the New Deal programs of the 1930s. If you give a shit about this, then go and Google it yourself, but make no mistake. Racial housing segregation was no accident and still has incredibly harmful effects to this day because generational wealth in the United States is almost always tied to real estate and home ownership. Blacks were formerly denied these opportunities and still are, at least to some extent. So anyone who says the effects of slavery and racism are in the past are, at best, deluding themselves but more than likely just full of shit.

So let's talk about Ray. He turned out to be a great kid despite my almost superhuman efforts to fuck it up. I wasn't exactly cut out to be a father, but had we not lost Linda, he would have had an amazing mother. I'm not using her loss as an excuse. I could have done better, but you are who you are and do the best you can. And Ray turned out to be a pretty damn good kid. He is bright, kind, and thoughtful but in a practical kind of way. And he is a good-looking kid, sort of a poor man's Bradley Cooper, although I doubt Bradley Cooper would consider it a compliment.

Ray is a lot more like Linda than he is me. And just like Linda, he's still a bit gullible. Soon after he got back from Vegas, he came to visit us at the codger campus, and me and my boys (Lenny, Sid, Alex, and Slick) were watching boxing on TV. Sid's wife was there too. Sid and Slick had wives living with them at the facility. Alex was a lifelong bachelor, and Lenny was a widower like me. Over the years, we would fuck with Alex relentlessly, suggesting none too subtly that he was gay. For the record, he isn't, or at least I don't think he is. To be honest, I just think he is one of those people who had no interest in sex or romance no matter who is on the other end of his dick. He's just happy to do what he wants, which was always to hang out with his friends and gamble his balls off.

Anyway, we are watching this fight when Ray pops in for a visit. One of the fighters was destroying the other, landing blow after blow. It was bad enough that Alex was saying "They should have stopped this fight before he kills this fucking guy."

Lenny looks over at Ray with a grin and says, "I don't think so. I think he's gonna make a comeback."

Ray took the bait, laughed, and said, "Would you like to put your money where your mouth is? I'll take a hundred bucks on that guy." He meant the one who was, at that time, pummeling the other schlep.

Lenny couldn't wait to accept the bet because we knew something that Ray didn't. The fight was on tape, a replay. It wasn't thirty seconds before the pummeled fighter started making an improbable comeback, landing shot after shot until the other fighter wobbled across the ring and into the ropes before landing face first on the canvas . . . out cold. Only Ray was surprised. We had all seen this fight countless times.

So he's a bit gullible and wants only to see the best in people—just like his mom. It is near impossible to say what losing Linda meant to me. I can't say I "loved" her. That doesn't cover it. I was her, and she was me.

In any meaningful relationship between two people, there is a third entity that is created by the pairing. It consists of the personality and humanity that is created by the best (or sometimes worst) parts of the two people. I lost two people on the day my wife passed. I lost her, and I lost that person that I had been when I had her in my life. It would never be the same. I would never be the same. In time I recovered, at least as much as can be possible after so great a loss. There were other women along the way, good women, but they were not her. No one could be.

So I leaned on Ray in ways that no child should ever have to be leaned on. He was all I had and, for a time, I lived in fear that he, too, could be taken from me at any second. So he was smothered a bit, overprotected, but most of all, I think I tried to find that friend and companion I lost when I lost his mother, and no one could ever live up to that. I pray to God that he never felt my disappointment that not even he could replace Linda, to fill that silent void that can never be filled.

As far as I could tell, Ray has not yet found his Linda. I know he had been with that girl Lee out in Vegas for a while. They had come for a few visits, and I got to know her fairly well, and she was great—beautiful, biting wit, and quiet confidence. But I never felt that she was his "one." Not that it's my place to say, but I always got the sense from her that he was her "Mr. Right Now" rather than her "Mr. Right." I wasn't surprised at all to hear from Ray that she would not be coming back to Allset with him.

But this new one, Little Orphan Annie—who was not at all an orphan, and she was a doctor, to boot—has some potential. I would never say this to Ray, but if I were a quarter century younger, I would have been all over her. She is brilliant, apparently some type of biotech research scientist. I have always loved smart people in general and women in particular. She is also good looking but in that sort of studious, non-threatening way that doesn't make every random cock in the room stand up. And even better, she plays poker, and she is damn good at it. She understands the game in much the way Ray and I do, which believe me when I tell you, is quite rare. That makes her incredibly sexy but also somebody I don't need playing in our game. If they break up, I will make it a point to tell Ray to only bring bimbos with deep pockets to our game.

But Annie didn't stop coming around. She would stop by sometimes not to play in the game or even come with Ray. She would hang out and watch or kibbitz, but mostly she would chat with the nurses and aides who would stop by the apartment.

I saw her talking to the administrator of the facility, a usually dour, serious woman, but Annie had charmed her. The two of them laughed and talked without any awkward moments or long pauses. This continued for weeks until I concluded that this was something more than friendly conversation. Annie is a scientist and a fairly socially awkward one at that. This was not just idle chatter.

When I finally asked her about it, she answered me with a question of her own. "Have you noticed anyone getting sick around here?"

She asked in the most serious manner I had ever seen her say anything, and I answered saying that I had witnessed nothing out of the ordinary. Residents and staff seemed normal, but there was one thing. There had been a lot of absences and turnover among the staff over the last couple of months, a lot of new faces. I asked her if she thought this was a problem. Was there something going on? Her answer was pure scientist. "I'm not sure, but I'm going to find out."

I started asking a few questions myself, mostly out of boredom. I mean, how much poker can you play? How much boxing can you watch?

The answers surprised me, even scared me a little. Among the staff members, almost every single one of them had been Ill recently or knew someone who had. I'm no scientist, but I know a trend when I see one, and there was definitely something out of the ordinary, especially when you consider that not a single resident had been ill in any unusual way.

I was sure that this was what Annie was looking into, and I finally asked her about it. Again, her answer was pure scientist. "What we have here so far is unusual and apparently correlated. What we don't have is causation, and that's what we are going to look for."

Now I was even more interested. I asked her if she thought it could have anything to do with her laboratory. For the first time since I met her, she looked pensive and less than fully confident. "Not on my side," she said. "We don't work with anything even remotely capable of this, but I have no idea what is happening on the other side, and it looks like I'm going to have to find out."

From her demeanor, I could tell she was going to need help —real help. She explained that her options were not great when it came to getting someone to look into this. She could call the FDA, which was at least nominally overseeing her project, but she had concluded that it was not worth trying. The FDA, because of budget cuts, had very limited resources. Worse yet, she wasn't sure if they had any oversight capabilities when it came to the work happening on the other side. She didn't think calling the Department of Defense would help much either. After all, what could she really tell them at this point? A few Black people got a nasty flu? But because she is apparently a fuckin' genius, she had another plan. She would track down and contact the leaders of the Nonya Tribe somewhere in Oklahoma. They could send someone in to snoop around. It was still their land, and as landlords, they had access to anything. If they contacted the DOD or the FDA, they would have no choice but to take it seriously.

As I said, Annie is a clever one, a keeper.

5

THE NOT SO NATIVE AMERICAN

My name is Tiger but not because I look or act like one. Apparently, when I was born, I cried in a way that reminded my mother of the sound of a tiger's roar. My mother and pretty much everyone else has called me Tiger ever since. It's not my real name of course. My real name is very normal and white-man sounding, but I am not a white man—or at least not fully. I am half Native American, a fact I was not even aware of until the twenty-fifth of my now thirty-five years.

My father was a white man and a good one, as a father and as a man and as a white man. I lost him just short of my twenty-fifth birthday. For some reason, that's when my mother decided to tell me the truth of what she called my "Indian heritage."

It actually explained a lot of things that I had never cared to think much about. For one thing, it explained why I didn't really look white, at least not white enough for some people. It also explained the fact that growing up, we never seemed to have to worry about money very much. Neither of my parents really worked. Dad was an artist and writer that sold almost none of his work. Mom was more than happy to make me the focus of her life, keeping me religiously in school and almost completely out of trouble. It was the shared money from our tribal casino operation that always supported us and allowed my mother the freedom to be such a huge part of my upbringing even after losing my father.

Once I learned of my actual heritage I wanted to know as much as I could about it. Our tribe was known primarily as the Lapannay. We had been the largest of a group of bands of indigenous Americans that were spread out across much of what is now New York, Pennsylvania, New Jersey, Maryland, and eastern Delaware. They had lived at peace with each other for centuries, that is, until the white man came. After their arrival, what I discovered was, of course, appalling.

The rest is, of course, a horror show of European expansion, humiliation, and most of all, disease. What most people don't know is that it was disease that killed the greatest number of Native Americans. Much of it was incidental but certainly not minded at all by the ever-encroaching Europeans. What most people also don't know is that some of the diseases that killed my people were intentional. The decimation of my tribe was most certainly intentional.

My people were a particularly difficult group to control and remove, so a resourceful American colonel came up with an exceptionally vicious solution. He gave smallpox-infected blankets to the tribal elders, supposedly as a peace offering. Our people had zero natural immunity to the disease, and it tore through us like wildfire. The few remaining members, mostly women, were then involuntarily and cruelly shipped off to Oklahoma, which by this point had become the landing spot for the survivors of any number of tribal massacres and forced relocations. It was also this same delightful American colonel who renamed our tribe as the Nonyas, presumably as a demented and psychopathic joke, as if to say, "There ain't hardly Nonya left."

But there are still about twelve hundred of us left, mostly in Oklahoma, and most of us want little to do with Allset, New York, the place of the intentional destruction of our tribe, our culture, and our lives. But it can't be denied that one good thing did come out of it: we still have our land there, almost six square miles in and near Allset, New York. That's what remains of the hundreds of miles that I and my kind would once roam freely and in peace, but some smart lawyers put a casino on that land with our permission, and that has made us financially stable if not outright rich. We also just leased land to a company that built a pair of laboratories that I am told are on the cutting edge of research that could help a lot of people. This makes me happy but does not even begin to make up for past wrongs. But hey, it's a start.

Pardon me for saying so, but fuck that American colonel, and fuck people who would kill so casually and completely. But the more I learned, the more I realized that history was full of people like Colonel Fuckface. I became interested in knowing what it was it about humans that so often created such monsters, so I earned a degree in abnormal psychology. I also dabbled in law enforcement as a volunteer deputy. I'm certainly no expert, but I suspect that was the reason I was selected to go to New York and find out what was going on in that laboratory that was built on our land.

Apparently, there were some peculiar illnesses in the town, and I was to meet with one of the researchers at one of the labs. My first thought was why she had even contacted the tribe. It would make more sense that she would consult her superiors, or if that failed, the U.S. Food and Drug Administration or the Department of Defense, which presumably oversaw the other side of the lab.

She had instead reached out to the tribal elders. There had to be a reason, and that was just one of the things that I needed to find out. Why send me? Well, nobody else in the tribe wanted anything to do with that place, so why not send the half-breed? That's me.

I'm not particularly worldly, and I haven't done a lot of traveling. I've never even been to New York, not even to our own tribal land, so on one level I was excited to see the home of my ancestors, but at the same time, there was some dread at the thought of walking the actual grounds of the massacre and desecration of our people.

I was to meet with the research scientist, who I discovered through my own research was known as Little Orphan Annie, and as far as I could tell, the name was meant as a compliment. She had been a part of a number of breakthrough treatments for diseases that don't normally get much attention, the literal orphans of the pharmaceutical industry. She had an impeccable educational background and reputation.

Initially I would be meeting her away from the lab in order not to attract attention. She had chosen the meeting place, an assisted living facility a few miles from the lab and just off our tribal land. I have no idea why that was the chosen location. At that point, I didn't really know much about anything. All I knew was that some black people were getting sick and that a respected scientist believed it had something to do with what was happening at a laboratory on our tribal land. I guess that's a good enough reason for a trip to upstate New York.

6

THE RAINBLOW COALITION

I like Annie—a lot. She is brilliant, dedicated, funny in her own unique way, and completely dedicated to her life's work, which is saving people's lives. Compare that to the life of my father and me.

We are not bad guys, but we have spent most of our lives figuring out ways to separate people from their money in one way or another. Plus Annie plays poker, and she plays it well. To be honest, she is not at my level yet or that of my dad, but I have little doubt she will surpass us both given enough time and experience.

Even with all these details aside . . . she's hot. She is a sexy woman and even more so because I don't think she even realizes it or tries too hard at it. Am I in love with her? I have no idea. I'm not even sure what the word means with the way people throw it around so casually. But I can say this: I would rather be with her than play poker. I would rather be with her than hang with my dad and our friends. That's saying a lot. I can also say that I hope there is a future for Little Orphan Annie and me. We shall see.

When Annie told me that there was something weird going

on at Springview, and in Allset in general, I didn't hesitate to take her seriously. I started looking and asking around. Not only were Black people getting sick at Springview, but a lot of the Black folks who were regulars at the Hope were getting sick too. Even worse, we had seen our first death. Whatever was going on was no joke. It was mostly a flu-like ailment sometimes leading to respiratory problems, and in one case so far, respiratory failure and death.

I took it as a compliment when Annie asked me what we thought she should do. She knew there was nothing going on at her lab that could even remotely cause this, but she had very little connection to the other side, and her demeanor told me that she at least suspected that a "bug" of some type had escaped containment.

We talked for hours about the best course of action. I finally suggested that we go talk to my dad. Obviously he was no scientist, but he had seen firsthand what was going on at Springview.

It was Annie's idea to contact the tribe, and my dad immediately agreed. He reasoned that if there really were an accident of some sort, the FDA and DOD would be so worried about bad publicity and covering their ass, they would screw things up. If it were just a coincidence, then there would still be no harm in contacting the tribe. However, if this were some sort of plan or conspiracy, a tribal investigator would have the kind of access that might take months for a government entity to work through. A tribal member can walk right in. it's their property. Yes, that was the way to go, at least for now.

It was my dad's idea for her to have her first meeting with the tribal investigator at Springview, safely out of view of the labs and under the radar, plus he could meet and speak with some of the victims and families to try to figure out what the hell was going on. The tribe told Annie to expect a man named Tiger, and he would be arriving within the week.

Nonetheless, before she met with Tiger, Annie would meet

with Gladys Jones, Springview's top on-site administrator. She was a Black woman in her early fifties. She herself had not been ill but had several family members who had a recent respiratory ailment. She was a straightforward, no bullshit type of woman, never afraid to give her opinion, no matter who does or doesn't like it. My dad and Gladys had butted heads a few times since he's been here, and she always held her ground with him. My dad might not admit it, but I suspect he respects her for it. After their meeting, Annie and Gladys planned to speak with Tiger to bring him up to date with everything that was known. Then my dad and his boys and I would join the party.

This would be the most peculiar meeting of the minds as I could imagine. Annie arrived right on time for her private meeting with Gladys, which took place in her office and lasted just over a half hour. Another half hour passed after Tiger was included.

Meanwhile, the rest of us had assembled in the dining room, which was empty except for a couple of servers. It was me and my dad along with his buddies Slick, Alex, and Lenny. Gladys, Annie, and Tiger finally joined us, and after a few minutes of slightly awkward introductions, it was time to get down to business though I'm quite sure at that point, none of us really understood what that "business" actually was.

Tiger had a slight deer-in-the-headlights look as he introduced himself to each of us. I'm not sure if he was expecting such a large group to greet him. Come to think of it, I can't imagine what kind of greeting he could have possibly expected. It's not like this kind of thing comes along every day. How often do you call someone who could not possibly know anything about an issue, tell them that Black people are dying from a strange ailment on your land, and want you to come here to meet a group of weird strangers to try to figure out what is going on? That type of thing doesn't come up too often. Yet here he was in a roomful of people consisting of a research scientist, a nursing home administrator, and an assortment of old gamblers and one of their sons.

If I didn't already know that Tiger was Native American, I wouldn't have been able to tell from his appearance. He was fortyish, a bit shorter than me, and had a stout but not fat kind of build. If I had to describe his shape, I would say he was built like a wrestler—and I mean an actual wrestler, not the steroid-powered giants on TV. He had slightly graying brown hair and dressed smartly but didn't look comfortable in doing so, as if he were used to things being more casual.

It was Tiger who spoke first. He spoke with a confidence that didn't match his fidgety and nervous body language. It was not surprising. I doubt very much that he had done much public speaking, even to a crowd as small and strange as this one.

"My name is Tiger," he said, "and on behalf of the Lapannay tribe of New York State, I would like to thank you for bringing this to our attention."

It was rather formal, and not a single one of us had any idea who the Lapannay were. To us they were the mysterious and almost always absent Nonya Tribe, owners of our favorite and only casino.

No one spoke for a few awkward moments until Lenny finally asked, "Who the fuck are Lapannay?"

If Tiger was offended by the comment, he certainly didn't show it. Instead, he answered.

"I am the Lapannay. My tribe is the Lapannay. The name Nonya was given to us by the murderer who killed all but a few of our tribe that survive today. It is an evil name bestowed by an evil man, but he and his evil are in the past. The question is what is happening now, and what are we going to do?"

It was, of course, my father who spoke up first.

"What do we really have here so far?" he asked. "We have

one dead Black person and perhaps as many as a hundred Black people who are sick. Before we go any further, can any of you think of a single white person who has shown any symptoms of this illness?"

The silence that followed told him everything he needed to know about the answer. Whatever was happening was only affecting Black people.

"So what we have here is a potential shitstorm in a lot of different ways . . . and it's a race, because who knows how bad this can get and how fast? So whatever we are going to do, it better be now, like today!"

Everyone in the room nodded in agreement.

Tiger said, "I'm not going to be screwing around. It won't be long before I get the authorities involved, but I'm going to start first with a routine inspection of both sides of the lab."

Annie interjected. "That way, it won't arouse any suspicion over on the other side. It will look like the tribe is sending someone to oversee their tenants. Tiger's even going to say that the tribe is considering some venture funding in the biotech field, and he is just trying to learn a little bit."

"You may not even have to alert the authorities," my father said. "If enough people show up at the hospital with strange symptoms, and people are dying, the hospital will report it to the CDC."

"Don't be so sure of that," said Annie. "Right now this doesn't look like anything more than a typical flu. The only peculiarity is that it seems to be affecting only Black people, and that can often be explained by proximity. I'm not sure that very many have even gone to the hospital. We may want to check on that."

Up to this point, my dad's friends had been silent and attentive. What happened next made me wish they had stayed silent.

Gene, or "Slick" as he has been called for as long as I can remember, is a really good guy. He's a retired engineer, amazing poker player, and has raised three good kids while being married to the same woman for nearly fifty years. If I had to guess his IQ, I would put it at somewhere around a hundred fifty. He is not a stupid person, but at some point around when he turned seventy, he decided he no longer had any use for a filter for what he said and to whom he said it. He simply didn't give a shit anymore. Most of the time it's pretty cool and funny but not so much now as he gestured at the people seated around him.

"So this little rainblow coalition we put together here, Black, white, red . . . fag"—he pointed at Alex—"what the fuck are we going to do about this?"

Not that it matters, but Alex isn't actually gay, as far as I know, but my father and his friends had always made comments like that, supposedly in good nature because Alex had never married. The point is that it was an astoundingly racist and stupid comment to make, and to me, the saddest part is this: I know there was not the slightest bit of malice in what he said and how he said it. Slick will tell you that he has nothing against anybody, and he doesn't have a racist or homophobic bone in his body. And he believes it. He would pass a lie detector without a fuckin' blip. He just grew up in a world where a gay man is a "fag," a Native American is red, and Black folks work in the kitchen or clean up after you.

I'm not offering that as an excuse, nor am I offering forgiveness because forgiveness is not mine to give. It is best to understand that these mindsets exist and persist whether we like it or not—whether even Slick likes it or not.

If Tiger or anyone else was offended by Slicks comment, they didn't show it. Tiger just answered the question softly and confidently. "I will do something about it" he said.

7

YEAH, IT'S REAL

My husband Earl was born, raised, and lived almost all of his way too short life in Albany, New York. To be more precise, I should say he grew up in Arbor Hill, one of three neighborhoods in Albany where Black folks were allowed to live. I say "allowed" because in those days, not all that long ago, there were only three areas of Albany where Black people lived: Arbor Hill, West Hill, and South End. I myself grew up in the nearby Black neighborhood of South End.

There were no specific laws that I know of that prohibited Black people from living where they wanted, but it was understood that those areas were where Black people lived. As a practical matter, if you wanted to live among the whites, landlords and agents would simply refuse to rent or sell to you. If you were daring enough to be "uppity" about it, they would just say, "Okay, we will rent to you," and then quote you some absurd price, five times higher than the going rate just to make sure that the message was sent. I don't know what would have happened if any Blacks persisted further, but I'm quite sure it would not have been pretty. Times have changed, but to this day, only Black people live in West Hill, and the white areas are still at least eighty percent white.

Most of the Black kids go to West Hill High School, which is also still mostly Black but a bit more diverse than it was back when I met Earl. His family was middle class by local standards. Most of the residents were factory workers and janitors. His dad was the first in his family to get a college education and was a hospital lab technician and a pretty good provider. Earl himself wanted to be a doctor, but the resources for that simply didn't exist. He was, however, able to work himself through college and follow in his father's footsteps as a lab tech.

When GeneWorks came along in nearby Allset, it became a great opportunity for Earl and our family, which by now included three kids: Barack, Booker, and Angelou. Obviously we chose the names based on people we admire, people in whose footsteps we would love to have our children follow. Earl himself was named after the great blues guitarist Earl King. Earl's dad was a big fan.

GeneWorks recruited Earl for the position of lead lab tech, which they assured him was the equivalent of the director of a small department. They need not have tried that hard. They were already offering more than twice the money Earl was earning in his current position. As they say, they had him at "Hello."

There were reasons for the apparently great generosity shown by GeneWorks. Their lease with the Nonyas and their deal with the state of New York required both a certain percentage of local hiring and fulfilling racial quotas, so for them, Earl was a homerun. He filled two requirements by being both Black enough and local enough. In truth he wasn't a perfect match for the job. He had little experience with biotech, cutting edge research and supervised only a staff of three in his current position, but he was well respected and incredibly dedicated. Even Earl, who tended to downplay his own skills and accomplishments, felt he was ready for this role. At that time, it was an incredible opportunity for Earl, our family, and the usually hapless town of Allset.

For a while it was an incredible blessing. Though he couldn't talk about the laboratory, Earl was fulfilled and excited about going to work every day. And the extra money certainly didn't hurt. We were actually considering moving to Allset, which was some forty miles away and about an hour's commute for Earl each weekday morning and evening. Real estate prices in Allset had risen but were still within our reach, especially when you factor in his new salary and the physical and financial costs of the commute.

We didn't think much about it when Earl began to get sick. It had started with what seemed like a cold. He was stuffy and tired with a little bit of coughing and wheezing. Illness like this was not unusual for Earl. He was borderline diabetic with high cholesterol and high blood pressure, none of which were his fault. He watched what he ate and kept his weight under control. His doctor had said that Earl had a genetic predisposition, and he would have to be even more careful than most people to take care of himself. To his credit, he really did try. Even with three young kids and a demanding job, Earl always found time for a little exercise.

None of that seemed to matter. Earl had caught this "cold" and couldn't shake it. It got worse and worse. He started having trouble catching his breath. By that point, the kids and I seemed to have caught whatever he had, and each of us had a few days of cold symptoms but had quickly gotten better. Earl did not. I forced him to go the emergency room where they immediately hooked him up to oxygen and admitted him. He was clearly more comfortable, but he wasn't going to admit that to me since I was the one who forced him into seeking medical care.

It immediately became clear that there was more going on

here than just a common cold. A chest x-ray followed by a CT scan revealed that there was something very unusual going on with his lungs. The doctors were kind but seemed to be perplexed themselves as they offered me their best guess at what was happening. The lung tissue itself seemed to be shrinking and breaking down on a cellular level, something they had seen before but only in patients with advanced chronic lung diseases. They offered little in terms of what his prognosis might be, and as it turned out, it didn't matter. That same day, his lungs literally gave out, and he was immediately moved to ICU and placed on a respirator.

The next morning, they allowed our three children and me to see him in the ICU. Without their saying so, I knew this was a sign that the end was near. It all happened so fast, I was not processing this in any kind of emotional way, yet I fully understood that I was probably saying goodbye to my husband for the last time. I don't think the kids knew that, and to this day, I am glad they didn't. There would be more than enough time for grief after he passed, which he did later that afternoon. There weren't enough of his lungs left to keep him alive.

I still didn't really feel anything. There was too much to do. Of course, my children needed me. Their father was gone, and they were already feeling the loss. There were preparations to make, people to call. I would find time for my own grief later. I wasn't even thinking yet about who, if anyone, was to blame. It just didn't matter at that time.

Later that same day, a man named Tiger asked to see me. He explained that he represented the owners of the land on which my husband's laboratory was built. He explained that since the factory had been built on land owned by the Nonya band of Native Americans, they had the right to enter the property at any time even if there is secret U.S. Department of Defense activity going on.

That moment was the first time it occurred to me that Earl's death might have something to do with his work. Tiger wanted to know about Earl's job and whether I had noticed anything strange or if anyone else I knew had gotten sick. I didn't know much, but I answered to the best of my ability. Looking back on it now, I was almost certainly in shock.

Before he left, I asked him what he thought was going on. He said he didn't yet know, but he was going to make it his business to find out. He offered his condolences on the loss of my husband and said this was clearly more than some common cold or flu. Whatever it is, it is dangerous, and it is real.

Yes, my husband is dead. I can't argue with that, but there is certainly something I can agree with. Whatever he died from is dangerous—and it's real.

8

THE WHITE INFERIORIST

I am not a white supremacist. I, Reagan Forrest, am a white realist. I don't hate Black people, but I will tell you who does: God. God does. God hates niggers. For at least a millennium, they have been enslaved, humiliated, colonized, lynched, and deprived of every opportunity that the white man has been given. That is just scratching the surface, and I'm not talking out of my ass here.

I am the director of operations for GeneWorks on what our employees like to call the "dark side" of our operation here in Allset, but I am no biotech scientist. My background is in history and sociology. I hold a master's degree from Harvard University in sociology, and I am one of only seven people on the planet with a PhD in African Studies; the other six are Black, so when I tell you that the suffering of Black people on this planet is even worse than you think, believe me.

The money that created GeneWorks is still a bit of a mystery, even to me. I do know that most of it came from run-of-the-mill, actual white supremacists and the normal set of assholes and people still fighting the Civil War, or so I presume. It was their access to venture capital that enabled me to create

GeneWorks, but don't blame them. I am the one who put two and two together, genetic-wise, and realized that this was possible. I've told only a handful of people what the true intention of the company is: that we could, in fact, create a virus that could target and kill virtually every Black person on the planet.

I also know that much of the money came from the corporations that normally worm their way into Department of Defense projects that work on more normal, but still pretty demented, biotech defense projects. They are basically ATMs for military contractors, and all of them will fight to get their pin and debit card—and they usually do. In this case, they think they are supporting research for a mild, short-lived virus that will make some future enemy sick, but not too sick, and then eventually peter out on its own without much medical or scientific intervention. The point is to gain an advantage in some sort of future sustained conflict or to take the fight out of some future terrorist group. That is, of course, not our actual goal, but more on that later.

Getting back to what I was saying earlier, you know who else hates niggers? Niggers. Niggers hate niggers. And yes, I am using the word "niggers" interchangeably with the word "Black." Blacks, because of their history, are the single most racist group of people in the world, not that I can blame them. And ninety percent of that racism is directed at themselves.

Some of it is obvious. Across the globe, they have created their own form of a caste system where the lighter skinned you are, the more respect and opportunity you are given. The darker skinned Blacks have it way worse than the light skinned pretty much everywhere. Generally speaking, the darker you are, the worse off you are, including and especially the United States.

Blacks are certainly racist against whites. Of course, we all know they have every good reason to be that way, but it doesn't change the fact that they are. If *you* lived in a country where you are denied every opportunity by white people, harassed by white police, and these fuckers are the same color as the people who chained, whipped, and raped your ancestors for centuries, how would that make you feel? Oh yes, Blacks are the most racist people out there. It may not be their fault, but they still have got to go.

This also applies to Black racism against lots of other groups. White people have spent centuries brainwashing Blacks into believing that every Jew is out to cheat them, and every spic and chink is going to steal their shitty-ass job pushing a broom for $349 a week—and that's before taxes.

Blacks are also the worst racists when it comes to arguably the worst form of racism, the so-called soft racism of low expectations. They have been so mutilated by God and history that they expect absolutely nothing of themselves, and that's usually exactly what they get.

There has been so much talk recently of "white privilege," and only the most stupid, racist, or delusional idiots would deny its existence. Am I murderous? Certainly. Visionary? I will allow history to decide, but for the record, I'm definitely neither delusional nor stupid.

I think that the Black racism of low expectation is caused by such a deep-rooted, beaten-in lack of confidence and sense of self-worth that no white person can possibly understand it. Never once in my life have I ever felt that I couldn't do something, live anywhere I want, or accomplish something that I set out to do. Few Black people start out with that level of confidence or expectation. We have taken that expectation from them over centuries of brutality, torture, and institutional destruction of their families and opportunities that goes all the way back to the days that we kidnapped them off the shores of Africa. We have spent centuries explaining to them exactly what pieces of shit they are and using every possibly way to show it, so much so that both Blacks and whites believe it themselves, if only subconsciously but to their core. None of this is the fault of niggers, but at this point, it is what it is, and they've got to go.

As I said, I am a historian, so I can tell you exactly why white Europeans took over the world and enslaved most, if not all, of the world's Black people. The short answer is . . . they had to. For many millennia, Africans, the first humans, lived in a vast land of relative peace and abundant natural resources. Their populations were sparse, separated, and were therefore spared the worst of disease and violence that go hand in hand with population density.

Europe, on the other hand, was populated by those who had migrated north from humanity's cradle of life in Africa over many millennia. The climate became colder and life more difficult the further north they would migrate. Over millennia, they formed kingdoms and fiefdoms and centers of population much denser than those anywhere else on earth.

This led to even more scarcity, inequality, and the need to fight for the right to live. It led to diseases borne of population density after which some would survive and build up immunity that no one else in the world would possess. They were forced to learn how to fight to survive, how to fight for their lord, their king, their country, or their supper. In other words, they needed to learn to kill. So they did, and by necessity, they were finding newer and better ways to do it.

I'm going to venture a bit out of my field for a moment. There is the age-old argument in the study of human psychology called "nature versus nurture." It poses this question: Are we born who we are, or do we become who we are because of our surroundings and upbringing? For what it's worth, I believe it is almost always a combination of both.

Bad genes can make a person a schizophrenic or sociopath, no matter what their upbringing, and obviously, a bad, painful, or abusive upbringing would make it even worse. I also believe that a person born with a normal psychology can be turned into a monster from horrific treatment during childhood. In other words, God makes us what we are, but a lot can change based on what happens to us once we get here.

We probably can't turn a born devil into an angel with an angel's upbringing, but we can turn an angel into a devil by treating him like one. There is no doubt in my mind that we have done this to a vast majority of Blacks. It's a shame. It's wrong. It's shitty, and it's in no way the fault of Black people, but as the saying goes, "They still gots to go!"

Now that brings up an issue that I may be the only person in the world to ever consider: Are European whites insidious, violent, enslaving, vicious lunatics representative of true human nature? Is it true that all humans are these horrible monsters at heart and in action, or do we just believe this jaundiced view of human nature because we have never experienced anything else?

White European domination of the world, its culture, and its people has been so complete and so long-lasting that we simply might not recognize that there is any other way to be. Maybe whites really are a peaceful, thoughtful, and kind species at heart that simply never had a world in which to behave that way. We simply know nothing else, and no other way has been tried during any of our lifetimes or that of our parents or grandparents or even our great-great-great-grandparents. It's an intellectual exercise at best, a question for which I will make sure we never have an answer.

It nags at me though. Ample evidence exists of peaceful, healthy, non-white civilizations scattered around the globe. Most, if not all, were destroyed over centuries of white colonization of the world. Don't get me wrong. Not every pre-colonial society was idyllic, pure, and nonviolent, but I think any historian worth his lily-white salt would have a hard time finding a pre-colonization civilization that was even close to as violent, power hungry, or resource-thieving as even the most benign of the colonialists.

And that's not even considering the Eastern world. Certainly they had their share of wars, kingdoms, and more than a few densely populated areas where disease and eventual immunity would occur. Yet there were virtually endless centuries of relative peace and prosperity leading up to the colonial era.

The point is, I think an argument can be made that the jaundiced view we hold of all humanity may not be true. We humans may very well be better than that. We may very well be better than the sick, violent, selfish European whites that came to rule the only world and culture we know.

Our true selves may be kind, magnanimous, and peaceful. And I feel just the slightest bit wistful that we will never get to know that for sure one way or the other because my work here at GeneWorks will kill or render sterile every nigger on the planet. We will have racial harmony because we will have one race.

As I have said, it is not because I hate Black people. On the contrary, I admire them. I pity them. I fear them. The actual triangular trade of Black African slaves ended in 1808 when it became illegal in both the U.S. and Great Britain. This was more than fifty years before the start of the Civil War. (Fun side note: the abolition of the slave trade was the result of the work of evangelical Christians on both sides of the Atlantic. It's hard to imagine our rabid modern evangelicals to be involved in such nonsense. These days, they would spend their time desperately spouting the biblical basis to justify slavery. They would be big fans.)

When white owners could no longer import new slaves, they turned to intensely breeding the ones already in North America. Thus began one of the greatest eugenics experiments in world history. As large and widespread as this experiment was, it is still little known or studied, nor are the results fully realized or understood.

The breeding of slaves was practiced prior to 1808, but became big business once it became illegal to import new ones. A new idea took root: why not breed them for the most desirable traits?

In the male, those traits were size, strength, and stupidity. In the Black female, the most desirable trait was fertility—and most likely sexual attractiveness to their owners who, in many if not most cases, would be perfectly happy to produce a mulatto slave offspring to add to the stable. Black women were bred *because* of intelligence, not despite it. It was useful in producing "house niggers" who could serve and perform relatively complex tasks. It explains quite a bit if one can remove the blinders of the politically correct and the polite, so I will say what everyone else in the world is afraid to say: Black people are better than white people in every conceivable way. As a rule they are: bigger, stronger, faster, more fertile and, dare I say, possess larger genitalia.

They dance better. They sing better. They are even smarter . . . study after study has proven this when one factors in the massive socioeconomic factors that have stunted their emotional and intellectual growth.

They are simply better in every measurable way, and that is why I must remove them. The white race has no chance. The built-in tilt of the field against Black people is leveling. They are making gains politically, economically, and emotionally with each minute that passes. And worse, they are beginning to realize it. The days of the nigger knowing and even feeling his place as hapless victims to a hostile world is fading with each sunset.

In the world that is coming, the white man will have no chance. The war is coming, and without me, the white race will lose and lose big. The white man will live on as slaves to an economic and political system that will be much more fairly balanced, and in such a balance, we cannot possibly compete, let alone win. So I will save us. I am the monster, the behemoth that wins the war for the white man that he cannot possibly win on his own. And I will accept any judgment passed down on me by God, history, or man—but the white race will live on.

Even I felt bad about Earl and not just because it is bringing us unwanted attention at a time we are not yet ready for it. He was a good man. He was hardworking and totally dedicated to the work that he thought we were doing. No one was supposed to die yet, but his exposure to the virus was too soon, too extensive, and he was far too weakened by preexisting conditions to survive.

I knew that we had already caused a "Black flu" in the area around Allset, but I also knew it would prompt few if any hospital visits and would not be seen as race specific for quite a while. After all, Blacks generally live with Blacks and associate with Blacks, so it's not abnormal for a small cluster of mild illness to affect a certain ethnic group. None of that would have raised eyebrows or brought scrutiny from the CDC or any other government agency, especially not the DOD. They only care that their contractors get paid on time and that they eventually get the product they are paying for.

However, I knew his death would bring attention from someone, and not surprisingly, it came first from the one they call Little Orphan Annie. She runs the operation on the other side of the lab. Technically she is an employee of mine, but I had no hand in her hiring. My only concern was that her side of our operation be as clear and publicly transparent as possible.

She made no official visit to our side of the facility. She knows better than that. We know each other casually and a little bit socially. As it happens, we are both poker players, and I have found myself sitting across a poker table from her on more than one occasion. She is a frequent visitor to The Hope poker room here in Allset. I, too, am somewhat of a regular. I probably visit two to three times a month.

Soon after the death of Earl, I found Annie seated next to me at a poker table. We, of course, knew each other, and I am sure she believed that I would consider this a chance encounter. I did not.

I knew she was fishing for information, but there was certainly no good reason to let her know that I knew, so we chatted amiably about poker with only the vaguest mention of our respective work. Even her own work was classified, and any shoptalk in that environment would have been a serious breach of protocol, so she was subtle. And I was receptive.

We both agreed what a terrible tragedy it was about Earl and that clearly it had nothing to do with our respective work. What happened next surprised me a little . . . but just a little. She invited me to the codger game over at Springview, and I accepted the invitation because, as usual, I knew some things that she did not.

Having the DOD in your corner has some advantages, and I had background research done on her and about thirty others involved both on my side of the lab and hers. This was just basic due diligence on my part. You always need to know with whom you might be dealing.

I knew of the codger game at Springview from the casino. Pretty much everybody knew about that game, but I also knew of her relationship with the casino executive, Ray Louis, who had recently returned to Allset.

I even knew some things that Annie and Ray probably didn't know. For instance, Ray's father Brian was something of a data analyst and had done some work with U.S. intelligence over the years. He also had a surprisingly high government security clearance that he maintained even now in his so-called retirement.

I wasn't particularly worried. There wasn't much they could know, but Annie's association with Ray and Brian was a cause for concern. Annie and Brian would be people who would know which levers needed to be pulled to cause alarm, which was reason enough for me to accept her invitation to the codger game. No doubt I would be picked clean of my chips by these crafty old bastards, but it would be worth my while to find out a little more about what they might know and their state of mind.

We were close to where we needed to be to make the dream of a white world a reality but not quite yet. A loud yell from Annie or Brian could cause a swarm of CDC, media, and other scrutiny that we were not yet prepared for, so it was worth going there to calm their fears, humanize myself to them and, more importantly, buy just a little more time. Just the couple of days between now and the game just might be close enough.

And then there is Tiger, a tribal investigator sent by the Nonyas to poke around. No doubt Brian, Ray, Annie, or all three had alerted the tribe. I had spent an hour with Tiger yesterday, touring our lab and showing him what I could without revealing genuine classified information . . . or my true intentions. We both knew that by the terms of our lease, he had every right to be there, but we owed him no access to classified information or materials.

Still, Tiger could be a problem. He was no scientist and had no clue what was going on, but he had that bulldog-type stature and a keen mind, telling me there was not going to be any quick or easy way to get around him.

I also knew of his trip to Springview, so I have no doubt that Annie had told him as much technical knowledge as he could grasp. Again, still no cause for real concern, but no Orphan Annie, nosy Indian, or old man was going to bring this down. No way.

I'm almost there. The dream is almost a reality. All I need is just a little more time . . .

9

SO WHO THE HELL ARE YOU?

I wasn't at all surprised when my dad asked me to stop by Springview, but I was surprised by the way he sounded. It was more like a demand than a request. That was just not his style. When I asked him why, he just said, "Don't worry about it. Just get your ass over here today before the game starts."

Usually, he would call all the time asking me to bring him things like beer, not that he couldn't do these errands for himself. He still has a car. He is certainly no prisoner at the assisted living facility. I think it just made him happy to ask me for stuff, and if I'm being completely honest, it made me happy to do it. He is still my best friend, and bringing him things was just a way for me to end up there without us being sappy about it and, as usual, it works.

This case was different. He sounded a bit confused and nervous and would absolutely not take no for an answer. If it were anyone else, I would have suspected illness or maybe the beginning of Alzheimer's, but this was Brian Louis, completely in control of his faculties and considerable talent and intellect.

Clearly, he wanted to tell me something. The only thing I didn't know was what it was, and I had no idea what to expect. He had made a point of telling me to be there today at 2:00 p.m., but I knew the poker game started at 4:00. I was coming to play that day anyway, so I knew he wanted to talk to me without a lot of people around.

I arrived at his place a little early. I schmoozed a bit with some of the seniors and staff in the lobby before heading upstairs to his apartment. When I got there, I found my father seated in his recliner with Lenny and Sid sitting on the adjacent couch. I walked in unannounced, and they barely acknowledged me.

They were busy. The three lifetime degenerate gamblers were watching a tennis match (live TV this time; I made sure) and betting with each other on every point—five dollars on each bet and keeping track of who owed who what so far. Even though I knew it was live, I wanted nothing to do with this action and just pulled up a chair from the poker table and sat down to watch, figuring my dad would get down to business when he was good and ready.

Tennis is a weird sport to bet on, even for them. It's especially weird point by point because the server generally has the advantage and, of course, these three all knew that. So they had a system (of course). They took turns initiating the bet and choosing the player they were betting on. The other two would take turns with one of the other two forced to accept the wager on a rotating basis unless the other person actually wanted the action. They were just having some harmless fun, killing time. Nobody would ever win or lose more than a hundred bucks or so, and it gave them a chance to have fun, yell at the players on TV, and fuck around with each other relentlessly, their favorite pastime.

It wasn't long before Dad was ready to talk, and he wasn't subtle about it. He pointed at Lenny and Sid.

"You two fucks gotta get outta here. I need to talk to him," he said, pointing at me. "We'll settle up later."

Lenny and Sid grabbed their phones and cigarettes and headed for the door.

Once we were alone, he motioned me over to the couch and turned off the TV. His entire demeanor changed instantly. Gone was the happy-go-lucky gambler betting on tennis. In its place was a serious man.

It was not completely out of character. I knew this Brian from when I would get a bad report card or if I disappeared when I was a kid without telling him where I was going. It's funny how our parents, even the best parents, can intimidate us well into adulthood. And truth be told, I really was a bit intimidated and had no idea what was coming next.

"Ray," he said, "there are some things you don't know." He leaned forward in his chair and turned to face me. "I never intended to keep secrets from you, but there are some things that I don't believe should be told to children . . . and then when you grew up . . . it just never seemed to be the right time."

This was a Brian Louis I had never seen before. He seemed distraught and weary and was hesitating between almost every word. I, of course, was eager to hear what he had to say. Yes, I was curious as to what he was going to tell me, but I also desperately wanted for this to be over and for his anguish to stop.

He took a deep breath before he spoke. "Your mother was murdered." He blurted out the words suddenly, rapidly and began to sob as if the act of saying those words out loud had made the grief of four decades real again.

For my part, I was too much in shock to be shocked. So many different thoughts and emotions swirled through my consciousness that I could barely feel any of them. I just sat and watched him cry for what felt like an eternity, but it was probably only a minute or two.

The one and only emotion I could identify in me was anger. I was mad that he had kept this from me for more than forty years, but there was more. By now he had regained his composure and continued.

"Your mother was a spy, at least that's what they call it in the movies. The truth was she was a first-rate linguist and occasional field operative. They had recruited her straight out of high school. Her murder was useless and meaningless, a last gasp of some desperate East German Stasi member near the end of the Cold War. She died of blunt force trauma to her skull, a favored tactic of Stasi assassins that liked clean kills."

I was too stunned to do anything but listen. There was not a word of this that I could have ever possibly imagined.

"Four days after you were born, I awoke to find her next to me in our bed, clearly dead but with almost no blood. Our agency promptly came and took her away and briefly scoured our house for any evidence of the perpetrator, but they already knew. We all did. At that point, our government wanted no publicity, nothing that might interfere with the anticipated downfall of the Soviet Bloc, so she was taken to a hospital and declared dead of a ruptured brain aneurysm, which was actually true. It just had not occurred randomly. There was no further publicity, no questions of the official autopsy. It was just over. Not even anyone in our family knows the real truth, until now. I couldn't tell anyone out of fear that I, or God forbid you, could become a target.

"Did you ever wonder how we ended up with the names Ray and Brian Louis? Yes, it's a tribute to Joe Louis, but it was no accident. I had our names changed. After what happened to your mother, I was afraid that something might happen to us. It was probably irrational, but it made me feel better at the time."

By then my dad was well past sobbing and had been speaking in a clear, almost matter-of-fact way. I had recovered from my shock and had been listening intently to each word.

Questions had begun to form in my mind, and I asked the first one that occurred to me.

"Dad, if all of this is true, and I'm sure it is, then who the hell are you? Who the hell are we? What's our real name?"

He reclined in his chair, fully back to his normal self, and answered calmly. "Our real name is Litvinov. My grandparents were imprisoned Russian dissidents, and I am exactly what I have always been and who you know me to be—but with one difference. I, too, had been recruited straight out of high school but as a data analyst. I have functioned in that role on and off for the last forty years. At this point, I am little more than an occasional contract consultant, mostly on issues that occurred before most of today's operatives were even born."

"Dad, I know all of this is painful for you . . . so why tell me now after all these years?"

His answer surprised me yet again.

"There is something fucked up going on at that lab," he said. "I'm sure of it. It's no coincidence that only Blacks are getting sick. A lot of the people I worked with over the last forty years are in positions of some power right now, so I can help. And I'm going to do just that.

"Ray, I know you like this girl Annie, and all of my instincts tell me that she is not in on this, that she is only there to put a pretty face on the operation, but we can't afford not to be sure of that, so I don't want you to breathe a word of this to anyone, especially to her, not until we are sure. I hope that doesn't hurt your feelings."

He paused for a moment before continuing. "Scratch that. I don't give a shit if it hurts your feelings. Just keep your mouth shut until I tell you otherwise."

I was a taken aback by the fact that we might not be able to trust Annie, but I was also happy. Brian Louis was back.

I would like to tell you that we hugged or had an emotional embrace. We didn't. What needed to be said was said. What needed to be done was now clear. We are simply not those kinds of people anyway. Besides, it was almost time for the poker game, and there were always sheep to be fleeced. It was time to set up for today's game.

10

A TIGER ON THE PROWL

It probably shouldn't surprise me, but it still amazes me that there are so many people out there with rabid anger about the fact that my tribe and many others have thrived financially from the casinos and other legal loopholes that have brought many of us some measure of prosperity. I say legal loopholes, but it is the law itself that grants us our reservations and some measure of autonomy. It seems ironic and justifiable at the same time. Wasn't it perfectly legal when the colonialists of Europe stole our land, desecrated our holy places, and turned us into foreigners on our own land? But when we use the current law of the land to gain some measure of security, self-sufficiency, and justice, we are called ungrateful opportunists.

Now I'm not saying we ourselves are perfect. We now suffer many of the ills that come along with affluence and power, emulating the repulsive behavior of our conquerors. There are so many painful examples of tribes working against each other to prevent new casino competition and using all the government's levers of power to make it happen. There are battles within tribes over who exactly is a member, trying to limit the number of valid members so fewer members receive even more of the cut for themselves. There has been corruption, dirty dealing, and even an actual gunfight in a casino between warring tribal members. There are a few tribes, particularly in Florida, that have used the awesome power of money and influence to virtually dominate the state and spread their influence worldwide.

In my mind, much of this is justified, but it pains me to watch us become just like those that have harmed so many. I don't like it, but I suppose it is still better than the alternative, a return to the days of hungry, homeless Natives, drowning in self-pity, addiction, and malaise.

All of this is true but now irrelevant to the job at hand. I was entrusted with finding out what was going on our land, and that is exactly what I am doing. My tour of the lab was uneventful, which was exactly what I expected. They knew I was coming, and if there were to be any rattling skeletons, they would have been safely locked away long before my arrival.

However, the director I met with was of some interest, mostly because I couldn't figure out exactly how he had or even wanted the job. Reagan Forrest was a bit of an enigma. Not a big or impressive man physically, he was about 5'7" with a sort of dumpy-looking frame, but he did have a head full of what looked like natural and very blond hair and bright blue, penetrating eyes, almost always a sign of a keen intellect. In my own research, I had discovered that highly specialized scientists, unquestioned leaders in their field, usually led projects of this type. This was an industry where decisions on the ground were made not by pencil pushers or MBAs but by scientists. And Reagan Forrest was no scientist, at least not in biotech.

I knew he had been at the forefront of the company's fundraising and financial operations, but rarely were those people ever on site, and it was even more uncommon that they would ever oversee day-to-day operations, so that alone made him a bit suspect. Why was he even here? He seemed friendly enough and showed me everything that the law would permit, but that question kept popping into my head. Why was he even here? There was no doubt he had a purpose and agenda for being here, but it was still a bit of a leap to link his enthusiasm for his work with homicidal or even genocidal intent.

I spent the day after my inspection talking to and meeting with as many of the victims as possible. Several of the staff at Springview shared stories of family members who were growing increasing ill—and it was spreading. Still, there had not been a single case I could find involving a white person.

It was becoming less and less likely that it was a case of proximity or that it was confined to predominantly Black neighborhoods. The Black staff at Springview was constantly interacting with the residents, and not a single one of the residents had shown any sign of the illness.

At this point, there had been three more hospital admissions that I knew of. None of them were in the ICU yet, but with four cases recorded at the hospital, I was guessing, or at least hoping, that they had made a report to the CDC, but it was of no matter. I knew enough to know that it was time to alert whatever authorities the tribal elders might have access to, which would be quite a few, so I reported back to the tribal elders what I had found so far. There was broad agreement among them that it was time to act.

Their decision wasn't made entirely out of altruistic good will. Something like this happening on our land could bring shame and unfavorable publicity for the tribe, and they would do anything to avoid that, so it was agreed that they would begin to alert the appropriate authorities. Technically, the Bureau of Indian Affairs is a part of the Department of the Interior, but as a practical matter, our elders had far more resources at their disposal than official channels. They would be able to reach the assistant secretaries of the FDA, State Department, and DOD, and of course, the CDC.

The elders left me little doubt that they would use every tool they had at their disposal. The irony of this statement is not lost on me. "The cavalry is coming." The only question is how long it might take.

Somebody, almost certainly GeneWorks, was intentionally trying to kill Black people. It is shocking, and I'm sure it would be shocking to anyone. Even the most hardened, racist redneck would probably have trouble getting on board with this. But to me it was more. To me it was no different than the use of those smallpox-infected blankets used to destroy my ancestors—shocking, disgusting, but sadly, quite believable. It was biological warfare brought into the twenty-first century, and I simply can't let that happen.

I was tracking down as many victims as I could and running down however many leads as I could find. They took me to several other nursing homes and assisted living facilities where I found much of the same effects there were at Springview: numerous illnesses were occurring among the Black staff and their families and none among the white residents.

But it had gone beyond that. I was finding fast food restaurants closed in the middle of the day with signs on the window saying they were temporarily closed for lack of staffing. Two local nightclubs that had largely Black clientele and employees had also closed without explanation. I could only assume that their mostly Black staff and customers were ill.

There were four hospitals in and around Allset. I visited all of them and found that emergency room visits had tripled, and there had been numerous admissions and more than a handful of patients in ICU, all of them Black people with similar symptoms. They even had a name for it—the Black flu.

I didn't ask, but at this point I was sure that the hospitals were beginning to reach out to authorities to report what was clearly now a highly specific epidemic. The final hospital I visited had already reported three deaths associated with the illness. I made an effort to follow up with the families, but all refused to see me, not out of malice but simply because all of those family members had themselves contracted the disease.

The authorities would be here soon, but now it was the time to find out a little more about this Reagan Forrest. According to my new gambling friends at Springview, the best way to learn about a man is to see who he is when he gambles, who he is when he wins and loses. They described this kind of observation as a microscope to the soul.

The poker game was tonight at Springview, and I would be there to see this possibly dark soul, hopefully unveiled.

11

BRIAN WHO?

I had not told Ray everything. There was simply no need to. So much of what I could have told him is just so dispiriting that I saw no need to burden him with it. A good bit of it is stuff I wish I didn't even know myself, not to mention that the knowledge could still bring danger, even to this day.

My work for the U.S. government has spanned nearly five decades. It didn't start out that way, but at some point, my work became something of a chronicle of the downfall of the American empire, mostly at its own hands.

I investigated and reported on dozens of instances of consolidation of power, money, and influence into the hands of a very few, most of them not elected. Corporations, the religious right, and military contractors had amassed and centralized power in a way that had never existed before.

It was really no one's fault per se. Technology, travel, and communication had made it possible for a multi-billion dollar company to be run from a broom closet in Delaware. Endless manipulated military conflicts became ATMs for the defense contractors who would use that power to even further control our elected officials. Telecoms, oil companies, and many other enterprises consolidated into massive behemoths against whom our elected officials couldn't stand a chance. One misstep or one wrong vote would get them fired, targeted for scandal, or primaried, so almost all of our politicians from both parties will toe the corporate line. An economist would call this "regulatory capture," where the regulated become so powerful, they overpower the regulators.

This happened a long time ago, and it can only get worse from here. I call it corruption, and it is at the heart of all that ails us. I wish to God I could fix it rather than merely observe it.

Do you ever wonder why virtually everything supported by the American people in poll after poll is ignored? Way more than half of us want healthcare for all, like every other civilized nation. Yet it has never stood a chance legislatively. The health care industry and especially big pharma are just way too powerful for that to be possible.

Everyone claims to be against illegal immigration, yet it has never been stopped. I have nothing against immigration, but the true reason that no one has ever truly acted to stop illegal immigration is very simple: corporations like slaves, and an illegal immigrant workforce is as close as you can get to slave labor (unless you count the millions of prisoners forced to work for nearly free in our prisons). If we actually wished to stop illegal immigration, it would be a simple matter—impose harsh fines on the corporations that exploit them. Eliminate the financial incentive on both ends of the transaction. That would do it! Game over! Of course, it would also cause wages to rise for American workers. It would eliminate the artificially suppressed wages caused by the exploitation of the virtually slave-like, illegal alien worker. Wages would rise naturally, but have you ever heard such a simple and utterly effective solution proposed by anyone from either major party? Of course not.

Such a person would be immediately targeted and their political career ended by their corporate masters.

Three-quarters of Americans support safe and legal abortion (not that anyone likes abortion), yet here we stand on the brink of having abortion once again become a harshly punished crime in America. It's all the more galling to know it will crush the poor, annoy the semi-affluent, and cause thousands of women to die. They might as well call it the "God wants to kill some horny chicks act," and it still will not prevent abortion. It will only criminalize and endanger vulnerable woman and health care workers.

The bottom line is that there has been a somewhat slow-motion corporate coup in our once great nation, and I am going to explain it to you. This may be boring to some, but you know what? Tough shit. It can't fuckin' hurt you to learn something once in a while.

The takeover began slowly, as most awful things do, in 1971 with what is widely known as the *Powell Memorandum*. Lewis Powell was a corporate lawyer and later a Supreme Court Justice nominated by Richard Nixon. In all fairness, Powell was not a terrible man and was intellectually honest and genuine about his beliefs. Unfortunately for all of us, his beliefs may have had some measure of validity at the time, but over the decades that followed, they led to a corporate takeover of the United States that now threatens the planet and all of us who live here.

He wrote something called the *Powell Memorandum*, which was basically a call to arms for business to stop playing defense and start fighting back politically against the Ralph Naders of the world and the people fighting to label tobacco as an unsafe product. He was even against seatbelt mandates. He was hideously, horribly wrong but not dishonestly so. In fact, he became a Supreme Court Justice with a record of distinction, even joining the majority on the landmark *Roe v Wade* decision that legalized abortion nationwide.

There was no way this man could have known in 1971 just how much power and influence technology would permit these companies to acquire. I like to think it would have changed his thinking, but this we can never know, just as our Founding Fathers could not have known how much wealth and power could be concentrated in so few hands.

In the 1770s, the rich were defined by owning two things: land and people, neither of which fit neatly on a thumb drive or could be managed efficiently from a broom closet in the Cayman Islands. There is simply no way they could have conceived of the type of wealth and power that could be amassed in the modern world. The very concept of the *limited liability corporation* did not yet exist, not even as a theory. My bet, and I never make bets lightly, is that they would have addressed this issue in the Constitution had they even the wildest dream it could ever be possible. But they couldn't and didn't, and now the United States is a wholly owned subsidiary of the corporate world and a handful of multibillionaires.

When Lewis Powell wrote that memo in 1971, he had some legitimate arguments. The rallying cry of the conservatives at the time was "What is good for GM is good for America." Whether you agreed with that sentiment or not, it did have some validity. You could make a healthy argument that what was good for GM, as a proxy for all of corporate America, was good for America—its communities, its workers, and its shareholders.

Nonetheless, whatever truth it held half a century ago is complete nonsense now because there is truly no longer an entity that can be called an American company. Institutional and foreign investors own the vast majority of these corporations, and they have no interest in our communities, our workers, our infrastructure, or even our environment. The corporate goal is now singular: *enhance shareholder value*. There are no "American" corporations anymore, only ravenous amoral beasts that must feed relentlessly and constantly on everything —right down to our skin and bones.

Lewis Powell was not a bad man. He held beliefs that while misguided, in my view, held some validity at the time. In my role as an analyst, I reported to various intelligence organizations, congressional and senate committees, and on more than one occasion to the President himself. I became pigeonholed to the extent that my work became more and more about monopolies and political, religious, and corporate consolidation of power and their effect on the body politic.

The Founding Fathers' philosophy was the very antithesis of power consolidation. They believed that the true government of the people required the checks and balances that would prevent any such dangerous consolidation of power. They could never have foreseen the massive power of the modern corporation and the modern billionaire.

What the *Powell Memo* started, the Reagan administration ran with. They immediately crushed unions and ended almost all Depression-era banking regulations, which led almost immediately to the so-called S&L crisis, which was, in essence, a massive wealth transfer from the poor to the already wealthy.

They launched a massive racial war against Black people with their so-called War on Drugs, putting millions behind bars. Prisons, oftentimes owned by private companies, would funnel part of the kickback to the politicians who made it possible, all the while funding and protecting Nicaraguan drug cartels that flooded Black neighborhoods with crack cocaine.

George Bush was left with this bag of turds and made something of an honest effort to turn it around, but the cost of the banking crisis caused by Reagan's corporate handlers still cost each man, woman, and child close to $3000 per person . . . in 1989 dollars. The drug wars had already put millions of its victims behind bars, and Saddam Hussein's invasion of Kuwait served as the pretext for an even further expansion of the military industrial complex and its power.

Bill Clinton, even as a centrist Democrat, continued the ongoing transfer of wealth from poor to rich since he owed his success to the same banks and firms that had installed the puppet Reagan. He proceeded to further gut our social safety net with so-called bipartisan approval. He oversaw an even further nonsensical expansion of the drug war while our prison population tripled—mostly with Black men—all while enjoying a nice cigar.

The illegitimate presidency of George W. Bush was the real turning point for two main reasons, both of which I had studied and reported on at length. First, longtime supporters of the Bush family in the Saudi Arabian government orchestrated the September 11th attacks. The 9/11 terrorists themselves were Saudi citizens and Saudi trained. Not surprisingly, President Bush used this as an opportunity to attack two longtime political foes of Saudi Arabia, Iraq and Afghanistan.

As I reported to a Senate select committee at the time, there were valid reasons to attack Afghanistan. We did need to topple the Taliban and prevent any further coordinated terrorist attacks. The attack on Iraq, however, was utter and complete nonsense, and virtually every member of our intelligence community knew it at the time, myself included.

I and almost all of my colleagues recommended the same thing: topple the Saudi royal family, those who had actually attacked us. They were also the founders and financiers of Wahhabism, the most extreme, violent, and dangerous form of Islam. Our reports were littered throughout Washington at the time. They went to Congressional committees, think tanks, Senate hearings, and even made it into the hands of the defense secretary and President himself. It was of no matter.

Their goal was clear. They were going to use this Saudi

attack on America in order to destroy the enemies of the Saudis, reduce freedoms of Americans at home via the almost comically named Patriot Act, and further enrich the defense firms of Halliburton and especially Blackwater, further tightening their grip on our elected officials.

The other lesser-known legacy of the George W. Bush era was the rise of ALEC, The American Legislative Exchange Council. Few people even know of its existence, but it affects your life in a big way. It's the reason your internet sucks dick and is about the thirty-fifth best in the world. It's the reason verified mental patients can walk around Walmart with a handgun. Simply put, ALEC is comprised of most of the world's major corporations and billionaires. They literally write laws verbatim that they then give to bought-and-owned legislators who pass them, often unread.

Obviously these laws are written to make them even richer and more powerful and have absolutely nothing to do with you, your safety, survival, or well-being. This may be boring shit, but I assure you that every word of this affects you, is killing many of you, and is turning this once great nation into a third-world country, one fucked-up, self-serving law at a time.

The placeholder presidency of Barack Obama gave rise to the newest fashion in racism and also brought into play the forces that would later make Donald Trump president. Trump's verbosity made it okay for us to display our racism in ways that we were unable to before. This solidified the power structure of the religious right and the old-school John Birch-style white supremacists into a solid block that could easily be manipulated into doing the bidding of the already, almost omnipotent corporations and billionaires.

I dutifully chronicled and researched all of this as I had always been well paid to do, mostly from my home in New York but now in my new home in Springview. My work was part of countless hearings and research reports in a myriad of agencies right up to more than one president, but it made no difference; it will make no difference. The battle is over, the corporate coup complete. I don't feel I have wasted my efforts. I did my best. These are natural forces of technology and corporate structure over which none of us have any control. Only a complete reimagining of what a corporation is can change the inevitable.

Nonetheless, what is going on now is a whole other thing. I believe that there are people trying to destroy every person of color in the world. I am just an analyst—and I am an old man—but I will not let that happen. I will use every resource, every connection, and every favor I have earned over a lifetime of public service to stop this. I will.

We will have this poker game, and by the time it is over, I will know if Reagan Forrest is responsible. And I will find a way to stop this fucker—even If I must put a bullet in him myself. I will stop him.

12

BOND, FORREST BOND

One might wonder why I would go to Springview to play poker with the very people I know are a threat to my plans and, truth be told, I ask myself that same question. Why would I do that? Do I see myself as some sort of James Bond movie villain? Am I going just to taunt my foils with my evil plans even while doing so poses a risk to those very same plans? No. Quite simply put, I am not *a* villain or *the* villain. I am the hero of this story, the martyr, the savior, the only man willing to do what absolutely must be done to preserve the white race and Western civilization. For whatever it is worth, I am the good guy!

Does that make them the villains, then, this motley assortment of used dildos who are in one way or another trying to stop what I am trying to accomplish for the world? No, they aren't villains either. They are nowhere near smart enough, powerful enough, or fast enough to stop what is already almost inevitable. You have to be dangerous and competent in order to be a proper villain. And no one in this group is even close to being up to the task.

I don't know which one of them called which government

agency. Probably all of them called somebody. The FDA, CDC, DOD, NIH, and even the Red Cross have been blowing up my phone for the last couple of days. To be sure, Tiger, Annie, or one of the dipshits from Springview have sounded the alarm loud and clear, far and near. And you know what? There has been a flurry of phone calls and emails over the last couple of days, but there is not one single fuckin' boot on the ground that wasn't already here. No one from any government agency will be here for at least two days, probably three, and when they do finally get here, they are more likely to focus on the hospitals and nursing homes than they are on me and my work. Anyway, by then my work will be complete or so close to finished that it won't matter.

So you might reasonably ask yourself why, with something clearly going wrong and people getting sick, there is no immediate and massive national response. There are three reasons really. And being the gentleman that I am, I will be happy to explain.

First, I don't know how old you are, but no matter your age, this is not the U.S. government you might remember from your youth. For that matter, we are not the citizens you might remember either. There was a time that the government response would have been so fast and competent that it would make your head spin, but forty years of tax cuts and government budget cuts have created a hollowed-out shell that can barely get out of its own way. They simply do not have the resources they once did and simply can't be there when we need them. And "we the people" barely notice and barely care. When we do care, we almost always blame the wrong people. We all watched as the city of New Orleans drowned with mostly Black hands on deck. The little we did blame was on the barely sentient George W. Bush and the Democrats. No one had noticed the forty years of government decay and corporate takeover that had led up to that moment. We the people also didn't care that much for what is touched on in the second reason.

In New Orleans, just as it is now in Allset, it was only Blacks getting hurt and killed. And let's be honest with ourselves for a moment. Nobody gives a flying fuck when Black people are getting sick and dying—not whites, not the government, not the media, not the American Red Cross, and certainly not the church or the fuckin' Boy Scouts. They are way too busy molesting children and supporting anti-gay policies. Not even Black people seem to give a shit when only Blacks are getting hurt, but just try to imagine even one not-so-cute white kid dying of an unknown illness in some bumfuck hospital in some bumfuck town. The media, the government, and several of the better-known Muppets would be crawling all over the place, but Black folks getting sick and dying just doesn't do it for them, especially right now, which leads us to the third reason.

Even though I know that in the big picture, Blacks are superior, I am still a proud, smart white man, and I have used every ounce of white privilege at my disposal to become educated, resourceful, and successful. I may not be a biotech expert, but I am a highly trained professional blessed with what you might call "street smarts."

I have also spent most of my adult life dealing with one hapless bureaucracy after another. I know exactly what to say and exactly what they want to hear to get what I want. They are no match for me. Perhaps they never were. Therefore, I was not worried about what could happen at the poker game, and even though this group of clowns are not villains, they are the enemy —and one should always know one's enemies.

Tiger, for example, is a competent investigator and earnest in his intent, no matter that his intent is misguided. It wouldn't even surprise me if he felt even more incentive because smallpox-infected blankets wiped out almost his entire tribe. That might tend to make one just a little bitter.

The nigger-doctor Annie is nothing more than a token to put a pretty face on our operation. She's an able researcher and not too hard to look at, but just like the rest of them, she is way out of her league.

Brian Louis was and is a solid intelligence analyst but nothing more. From what I understand of his history, his murdered wife might have been more of a threat to me had she lived, but she didn't. An East German made sure of that decades ago. But in this situation, Brian Louis is barely more than the old, degenerate gambler he appears to be, and what he appears to be isn't even who he really is.

His real name is Litvinov, a name he changed four decades ago after his wife was murdered, probably out of fear of the people that killed her. No matter. He cannot harm me, no matter how high his connections nor how old his relationships within the intelligence community are. It's just too late.

As for me, I am what I am, and I will let history be the judge of that. But I am also a poker player, and the idea of playing in this game is something of a lifelong dream. I will be playing with some amazing players for the highest stakes imaginable. At least they will think so—and that will be more than enough.

13

THE GAME OF GAMES

I have spent most of my life in casinos, first The Hope and then at least a half dozen casinos I worked at throughout my ten years in Vegas. After that, God only knows how many other days I spent in casinos all over Vegas, Reno, and California. I have played in thousands of poker games and probably watched thousands more, but there is nothing in my experience that could compare to the game we have planned for today.

Poker is all about money, and money means a lot, but today the money is meaningless. Of course, the pride of winning still means something to me, and I would like nothing better to than to fleece these old fuckers right in their own back yard, yet even that was secondary. The stakes in this game were higher than anyone could imagine. At the time, even I could not have known just how crucial those stakes were.

I HAD a feeling Dad knew a lot more than he was letting on, but even without knowing every detail, I knew lives were on the line. Maybe I'm being melodramatic, but I believed the fate of the world was in jeopardy, so I was not under the illusion that this was just another poker game.

Dad had a very specific set of instructions about how he wanted this game to go and what he expected out of each of us. The players would be pretty much the usual roster—except for Forrest, of course. The lineup was going to be me, Lenny, Sid, Alex, Slick, my dad, Annie, and Forrest.

Tiger would be there also, but even though his tribe owned a casino, he had never played a hand of poker in his life. He would be the most interested of observers. That day, we were also going to use a dealer, which was not that unusual. Some days we would just take turns dealing. Other days we would have this guy Kirk deal the game. He was a Black kid in his mid-twenties, and he worked as a janitor at Springview. The boys had taught him to deal in his spare time, and he seemed to enjoy it. He certainly enjoyed the couple of hundred dollars in tips he would earn in a few hours of work in his off-hours.

I knew it was no coincidence that we would be using a dealer that day and even less a coincidence that the dealer would be a Black man. It was certainly part of the plan of the increasingly mysterious Brian Louis.

Dad wanted to draw Forrest out. He was under no illusion that Forrest could be tricked or cajoled into revealing whatever his endgame was, but Dad believed he could learn a lot about the man from how he played poker, in the way he conducted himself under pressure.

Poker has a way of revealing a man's soul in a way that nothing else can. Personality traits, even many subconscious ones, always seem to rise to the surface. You can learn from the way players handle their chips and cards. You can learn from the way they treat a waitress. You can learn a lot from how they treat the dealer. Do they blame the dealer for every lost dollar while reserving the glory of winning hands for themselves?

You can also learn just as much about a person from how

they win as how they lose. Are they a gracious winner, a sore loser, or both? There is so much to be learned at a poker table that I would not be surprised if Freud himself was a poker player. All of this learning means even more to me and my dad because whatever you want to call it, we still have our gift, our special talent.

The game itself would be a relatively low-stakes affair, one to two dollar no limit hold 'em with an initial buy-in of only two hundred dollars. Players could replenish their chips at any time as long as it was in between hands and did not exceed the table buy-in max of five hundred dollars.

By our standards, and I'm sure by Forrest's too, it was a pretty pedestrian game, but that wasn't really the point though, was it? The game would operate under its normal conditions, which for us meant it had a set starting and ending time. The game would usually be played every day except Sunday, with a cancellation here and there, but the time was almost always the same 1 p.m. to 6 p.m., a really short game by most players' standards, but remember, we're dealing with a bunch of old men with enlarged prostates.

My dad also had specific instructions: we were all to "play him soft" for the first two hours. By that, he meant we should let Forrest win. He also cautioned us to be subtle about it. Forrest is no dummy and would surely notice if we were tossing away winning hands and throwing money at him.

After that, it would be time for Forrest to lose—and lose big. The focus of the game from that point forward would be to strip him of every chip he had on the table and every dollar he had in his pocket, and in this phase, my dad didn't care if we were subtle or not. We would gang up on him and make sure he would lose. Part of this poker psychology experiment would be to see if we were able to take all the money he had on him. Would he ask to borrow to stay in the game? In itself, borrowing to gamble will tell you a lot about a man.

This was a poker game within a much larger game—part poker and part psychological profile. Quite possibly, it would be a fight for the soul and future of humanity. Several million hours of poker experience would be in that room, but I'm pretty sure none of us would have ever seen a game quite like this. We were as ready as we could be. The could-be spy Brian Louis made damn sure of it.

Forrest would be given seat three at the oval of the nine-player poker table. As usual, Brian Louis had a good reason for this. Seat three was on an angle from which, if a player wasn't careful, the players in seat two and four might be able to observe his hole cards. There was also a nondescript decorative mirror on the wall adjacent to seat three. If Forrest were lazy about it, then pretty much anyone in the room would see his hole cards in the reflection.

These codgers can't read a menu in a restaurant or see across the street, but I learned the hard way that if you got lazy with your cards in seat three, the old bastards would see them. Forrest would need to be very careful to protect his hand from view, and in case you don't know poker, players knowing what cards you hold is deadly and would make it impossible to win.

Don't get me wrong. We were going to take this fucker's money one way or another, but if he wasn't careful, he would make it very easy for us, and even that would tell us something about the man. Whether he knew the proper way to view his hand safely without risk of revealing it to others would show another glimpse of who and what he was, however small it might be. It all matters.

There's another thing you should know about poker: pretty much everyone who plays poker thinks they are good at it. I doubt Forrest would be any different. However, the truth is, in the long run, almost nobody wins, at least not in a casino.

Not to bore you with details, but the costs of poker in a casino are subtle but real and devastating for most players.

Statistics consistently show that less than two percent of casino poker players are long-term winners. All of the rest lose, yet if you went around any casino poker room and asked the players if they win more often than they lose, more than half would probably say yes, which is completely impossible mathematically. It's like the World Series of cognitive dissonance. Of course, in the Springview game, there is no rake or fee for the house. The only expense for the players is whether we tip the dealer on the occasions that we have one, like today.

Poker is a game of chance and skill with the odds stacked against you. On this day, there would be no chance for Forrest Reagan. Brian Louis would make certain of that.

14

THE LIFE INSURANCE SALESMAN

I had once again missed breakfast in the dining room. Breakfast was really not my thing. I'm rarely hungry in the morning, and I have a pretty simple habit that has served me well over the years: If I'm not hungry, I don't eat. Seems pretty simple, right? But I bet if most people really thought about it, they would realize that probably half the time they eat, it's not because they are hungry. Maybe they eat because it's just time to eat. Maybe they are bored. Maybe they are stressed and inhale a quart of ice cream, and it makes them feel better.

I'm not judging anyone. Over the years, I've held a few extra pounds on my frame from time to time, but eating only when I'm hungry has kept me pretty much out of trouble—no diabetes, no high blood pressure, and normal cholesterol. Not too bad for an old man, if I do say so myself.

WHEN THERE'S a knock at the door, I open it to a grey-haired man who looks to be pushing 60. He's holding a clipboard and wearing a pink polo shirt emblazoned with a large slogan that reads "SureLife for Life Insurance." The clipboard he holds is stuffed with flyers and some very official-looking documents. If you have never heard of SureLife Insurance, there's a pretty good reason for that. It doesn't exist.

The salesman walks in as I shake his hand and then pull him in closer for a brief hug.

"It's good to see you, Brian," he says. "Now, would you care to explain to me why I just spent the last half hour schmoozing people even older than you, trying to sign them up for insurance that doesn't exist?"

"You know why," I answer. "I'm being watched, and this fucker almost certainly knows who I am. I hope you put on a good show."

"No worries," he says. "I'm pretty sure I could have made a couple of actual sales if I really tried. So how long has it been, Brian? It's gotta be like fifteen years since I've seen you. Still a degenerate?"

"The worst," I answer. "You look good, man, and I'm really glad you're still in the shop. This is a big deal."

"I figured it had to be because this is a pretty big ask," he says as he produces a tiny device from his pocket. "There are like fourteen of these on the planet. It doesn't look like much, but it's beyond cutting edge. It will copy every morsel of data off of any system in seconds. After that, you can plug it in to any phone, and it will transmit that data as fast as the connection will allow. Just so you understand, if I plugged this into the NSA's mainframe, it would copy everything in less than fifty seconds. Everything. I will set up a dedicated system and phone number to receive the data so when you plug it into the phone, it should take three to five minutes to transmit, depending on the size of the database and assuming there's a decent wireless signal."

"Thank you," I reply. "Other than from me, have you heard

anything at all about this dipshit or what's going on at GeneWorks?"

"No," he answers, "and that should worry you. That means either the DOD isn't taking it seriously, or worse, he's got some real juice somewhere up the line. I don't understand. Why don't we just pop this motherfucker and be done with it?"

"Believe me, I've thought about it, but at this point. I don't think it will do us any good. Whatever he's got planned, he's close. We might need him alive, but once we get his data, it will be a different story. We'll see. And thanks again. You were always one of the good guys."

"Brian," he says, "I'm glad I got to see you today. I know it's been a long time, but I still think about Linda to this day. I'm so sorry about what happened. I can't help but feel like I could have done more to . . . "

"You couldn't!" I interrupted him a bit more abruptly than I mean to. "There's nothing any of us could've done. All we can do is to keep doing what we always do: protect this country from itself."

MY COLLEAGUE LOOKS like he is going to say more but thinks better of it. "I'm just sorry Brian. That's all. Here is the phone number for the data connection," he says, handing me a piece of paper. "Don't fuckin' lose it, old man."

He smiles. "Good luck and happy hunting."

"Thanks," I reply, "for everything. Now get the fuck out. I don't need any insurance."

Again he smiles, then turns and leaves, closing the door behind him. I still have one more phone call to make, one more favor to ask.

15

SHOWTIME

It's not quite true that I have never seen or played poker before. My second day in Allset, I visited our tribal casino's poker room and got an incredibly quick lesson. I watched a couple of videos about poker on the plane from Oklahoma and then watched a live game in our poker room for about half an hour. After that, I foolishly thought I was ready to give it a try. About forty-five minutes and three hundred dollars later, I realized there was much more to poker than meets the eye.

For one thing, it has its own language, a language for which I have the vocabulary of an infant. Check, raise, call, fold—that's just the tip of the iceberg. Are you "running hot" or did you take a "bad beat" and get "snapped off"? Are you the "cut off" or the "big blind" or "under the gun"? There are hundreds of poker terms that I still have no idea what they mean.

NEVERTHELESS, I considered a loss of three hundred dollars to be a relatively cheap lesson. I was not a complete novice coming into the game at Springview but still pretty close. It's a good thing I would be an observer rather than a player.

We all knew that Forrest would arrive early for the game, and he did—a half hour early to be exact—but we were ready. All of us had gathered in Brian's apartment at noon, right after a pre-game lunch and briefing in Springview's dining room.

Brian Louis had taken charge. He had given specific instructions to each of the players in the game. Listening to his briefing, I was again thankful to be watching this game rather than playing in it. A part of me even felt a little bit sorry for Forrest. He didn't stand a chance. Brian Louis was leaving very little to chance.

Brian, Ray, Ann, Slick, Alex, Lenny, and Sid were already playing when Forrest arrived at the apartment. Brian had wanted to have the game in progress when Forrest showed up. He had explained that it would be less awkward for everyone, plus it would leave only one chair open at the table, which was the seat Brian wanted Forrest in for reasons I don't completely understand.

Forrest arrived with little fanfare. The players barely acknowledged his arrival as he walked in through the open apartment door to the sound of chips and table talk. No one batted an eye, and the game just went on.

LEFT WITH LITTLE CHOICE, Forrest announced his arrival. "Hey guys, I'm Forrest Reagan. Thanks for the invite."

He trailed off a bit as he spoke when he realized nobody seemed to care. All he got was nods from a couple of the players and an extended hand from Brian Louis, gesturing toward the only open seat at the poker table.

Annie glanced in his direction and said, "Hi, Forrest. Have a seat. Buy-in is two to five."

She was referring to the buy-in to the game, between two to five hundred dollars. Forrest just nodded and reached for his wallet as he sat in the only available chair.

A hand was just ending as the dealer pushed a pot to Sid, who smiled broadly as he pulled in the chips. Sid flipped three one-dollar chips to the dealer and said to Kirk, "Here you go, kid. Buy yourself a sense of humor."

Kirk almost smiled as he tapped the three chips on the edge of the chip rack before dropping them into a small plastic tub that sat on the floor between his feet. Turning to our new player, he spread out the five, crisp one-hundred-dollar bills that were Forrest's buy-in, the table maximum.

"Five hundred dollar buy-in," announced Kirk to no one in particular but was a nod to casino norms and certainly not necessary in this environment.

Forrest straightened himself in his seat awkwardly as he received his chips. "Do I need to post, or should I just wait for the big?"

IN POKER LANGUAGE that I more or less understood, he asked whether he needed to post his blinds out of position to enter the game or wait until he was the big blind. Rules of this type are far from universal, and Brian settled it quickly.

"You are our guest. You don't need to post. Deal him in, Kirk."

And just like that, Forrest Reagan was in the game and receiving his first two hole cards for his first hand.

To a novice watching a game, poker almost looks like a team event with everyone working together for a common goal. Nothing could be further from reality. It is a bare-knuckle, all-out struggle for survival with an ever-shrinking supply of resources as the house removes its cut. It's a battle for pride, ego, and most of all, money. Not to get overly philosophical, but it is a truly American game in that it is a microcosm of the uniquely American life and mindset. That life is an endless and ruthless quest for more—more money, more things, more prestige—while in the end, the only real winner is the house.

For now, none of that mattered to Forrest. He found the game welcoming and the poker gods benign. Just as Brian had planned, Forrest was off to a great start. It was then that I realized the significance of putting Forrest in seat three. From where I was standing, I could see the faces of the two cards Forrest was holding.

IT'S NOT that he was being careless. Most savvy or professional poker players will look at their cards with both hands overlapping each other and over the cards. Then they'll use one or both thumbs to lift the corner of each of the two cards just enough to see the value of the cards.

Forrest also used this method, but he would lift the edges just a little too much, enough that I, and probably at least two or three of the players, could see them in the reflection of the harmless-looking mirror. He would indeed have no chance in this game.

At this point, barely thirty minutes into the game, he was already winning a pretty good amount. His original buy-in of five hundred had swelled to over a thousand in chips in front of him. As Kirk dealt each player their hole cards, Forrest looked down to find himself holding sevens, the seven of hearts and diamonds to be precise. It was a good but not dominant hand that I found tricky to play in my admittedly modest experience.

The trouble with a hand like that is even though you probably have the best starting hand at the table, if any of the five common board cards are higher than a seven (an almost statistical certainty), there is a good chance someone has made a pair higher than your sevens. It's the reason most experienced players will raise with that hand pre-flop in order to thin out the field and lessen the possibility of someone making an overpair, which is exactly what Forrest did.

HE MADE a raise to seventy-five dollars. I learned later that this was probably an excessive raise but certainly not a terrible play. And it got the desired result. Only Annie and Sid called the seventy-five dollar bet before the flop

As I said, two sevens in the hole are tricky to play. Even if one of the board cards is a seven, and you flop three of a kind, there is still the small but potentially disastrous possibility that one of your opponents holds a higher pair in the hole and also made three of a kind on the board. This doesn't happen a whole lot, but when it does, it can cost you everything you have in front of you. That situation, which the pros call "set over set," is dangerous because almost no one can fold with three of a kind, and there is only one remaining seven in the deck to potentially bail you out. It's about a forty-to-one long shot.

But that's not what happened here. The board was a rather pedestrian king, nine, and four, all different suits. For Forrest, the board brought no fear of a potential flush and a small but possible chance that one of his two remaining opponents in the hand could make a straight with the two common board cards to come. The immediate danger was that one of his opponents could have made a pair higher than his sevens, which had obviously not improved with the flop.

Even among pros, a variety of opinions exist about how to play this hand. Many would check (decline to make a bet) and fold to any bet from any remaining opponent, believing that they had made a pair higher than your sevens. You could make a modest bet, say fifty dollars or so, just hoping no one made any hand and would fold to even a small bet, or as Forrest did, you could make a large, aggressive bet.

He bet three hundred dollars, more than what was already in the pot. After all, he was on a roll. Every decision he had made so far was a good one, so why not be aggressive? A three hundred dollar bet was most certainly an aggressive one.

Sid was next to act and immediately folded his hand. That left only Annie standing between Forrest and another pot. I knew Forrest held only two sevens and from her seat at the table, I'm pretty sure Annie knew as well. They had never told me about it, but it wouldn't surprise me if they had worked out some system where the players who could see the cards Forrest held could signal that information to any player remaining in a hand with him.

Meanwhile, Annie had watched emotionlessly as Forrest meticulously cut out three hundred dollars in mostly red five-dollar chips to make his bet. He had larger denomination chips in front of him though. He could have easily used those to make the bet simpler and faster, but the mini mountain of chips made for an impressive display, a show whose meaning was not lost on Annie or the others, I'm sure.

AT NO TIME did Annie look down at her own hole cards. She simply sat motionless for what seemed like forever, and to Forrest, it must have seemed even longer. In reality it was only a few seconds, fifteen at most.

"I call," she said as she casually and efficiently flipped three hundred-dollar black chips a few inches out in front of her. Kirk quickly dragged her three chips and Forrest's stacks into the now very large pot.

Kirk tapped the table, burned the next card off the deck,

and then revealed a Jack as the turn card. This card would make the hand Forrest held even shakier. There were now three cards on the board higher than a seven and, even worse, made a straight a possibility. No one spoke, and all eyes were on Forrest as he stared at the board and then brought his hands together to once again view his hole cards. They were still sevens.

"I check." He breathed almost silently.

"Check?" asked Kirk just to be sure.

"Check." Forrest repeated the word just a little louder.

This, even I knew, was a rookie mistake. Forrest had fired hard in the first two betting rounds, representing strength. To decline to bet at this point showed weakness in a hand that now had a pot of almost a thousand dollars. It was up to Annie to check or bet, and she had the slightest look of surprise, almost as if she expected better from him. She could easily have taken the pot from him at this point, but that wasn't part of the plan.

"CHECK," she said loud and clear, tapping the table in front of her as she spoke.

Forrest stared intently at the four community cards as the river came off the deck. And even watching the fifth card come off is in itself an amateur move. A pro would be watching their opponents face as the card came off. After all it wasn't going to change. It would still be there to look at later. It was a harmless-looking deuce. He leaned back in his chair and seemed to regain his confidence. Only a few seconds passed before he announced firmly and maybe just a bit too loudly, "I'm all in!"

He started pushing his remaining chips toward the center of the table, again an amateur move.

"Hold on," said Kirk, stopping him before Forrest's chips

became mixed with the ones in the pot. "I need to know how much is there."

Kirk started breaking down the stacks but did not announce an amount. He would wait to see if Annie would ask for the count. She didn't.

"I don't know about this, Forrest," she said almost teasingly. "I've got a pretty big hand here."

She turned both of her cards face up, a tactic sometimes used by players when they are the last to act and facing a bet. She had not yet announced if she would match his almost seven-hundred-dollar bet. Her hole cards were an Ace and a King, so her official hand was a pair of Kings. If she chose to call his bet, she would win the hand. The board being what it was, his hand was little more than a poor and transparent bluff. Of course, Annie knew she was winning the hand, but again, that wasn't the plan. She was going to let him win, and he would never know the truth.

"I GUESS YOU GOT ME, FORREST," she said as she flipped her cards face down toward Kirk. "I fold."

An audible exhale came from Forrest, who had stopped breathing while awaiting Annie's decision. He smiled broadly as he reached for the pot that was now his. Even with both hands, he couldn't bring in the whole thing. Kirk helped, pushing the remaining chips in his direction.

Triumphantly, Forrest turned his two sevens face up to reveal what he thought was a brilliantly orchestrated bluff. He smiled in the way a mischievous boy might after getting away with a childish prank.

Surely, Forrest must think he belonged here. After all, these people weren't so tough. Everybody at the table acted suitably surprised and impressed. Thinking back on it now, it was almost funny.

There was no doubt Forrest believed he had pulled something over on Annie. He was joyful, gregarious even, as he threw a twenty-five dollar green chip towards Kirk, a generous tip even for a big pot.

"Here you go, kid," he said to Kirk and looked at him just a moment too long, almost as if he expected this Black kid to genuflect for such a fine tip.

Kirk replied with a simple glance and a professional "Thank you" as he tapped the tip on the edge of his bank and then dropped it in his tip bucket.

Annie poured it on. "You got me there, Forrest," she said. "Now it's gonna be Ramen noodles for me until payday."

"No worries, my dear," he replied with a genuine smile. "In a world where beauty is currency, you will always be quite rich."

I could see that Annie was genuinely flattered by the remark, and it occurred to me in that moment that as much as things change, some things don't. Annie was, in fact, a beautiful woman, not a fashion model, for sure, but at the risk of being sexist, I would say she is a solid eight, but here we have this incredibly accomplished woman in her prime still at least slightly wooed by the most superficial flattery imaginable. It wasn't that long ago that there would have been no Ann Byron, the respected research scientist. There would have only been a Black woman judged unworthy by the color of her skin or worthy by the shape of her body, the outlines of her face.

In my culture, women are honored throughout their lives. In Western culture, women are honored and paid attention to as long as they remain "hot." A woman without sexual appeal is without value and practically invisible, or so it appears to me. A woman without sexual appeal can only be noticed if and when she then competes as a man. Even then, no matter how successful she may become, she is then criticized for being "mannish" or a "bitch." It is a game women cannot win, even now.

Sid broke the momentary spell. "What a bag of horseshit!" he said with a laugh. "If I could say something like that with a straight face, I would have worn my dick out by the time I was thirty."

Even Forrest laughed as the players moved on to the next hand. Annie held a wry smile, shaking her head, not at all phased by these old boys being boys. The next hour or so went by with more of the same. Forrest couldn't lose a pot if he tried. At one point, he was up nearly four thousand dollars by my count.

There wasn't a particular moment I could point to when Brian decided it was time to turn the tables on Forrest, but it wasn't long before his stacks of chips began to shrink. It was clear to everyone in the room except Forrest what was happening. Springview had turned into what in the old days would be called a "clip joint," a casino or card room where you don't stand a chance. Forrest had been laughing and joking as the stacks of chips had grown, but as the chips evaporated, so did his good spirits and better judgment.

In poker there are tight players and loose players based on how many hands you get involved in. In modern Texas Hold 'em poker, there is no ante, so the player has no investment in the hand unless they are in one of the two "blind" positions where you must place a bet prior to receiving the hand in order to stimulate action. In most hands, in most games, players usually fold before investing any money in the pot. They simply fold and surrender their cards before the first bet. The looser a player is, the more hands they tend to invest in. The tighter a player is, the fewer hands they will play. As a very general rule, better players tend to be tight and have a higher threshold for what they consider to be a playable hand, worthy of a bet or call. Most recreational players fall somewhere in the middle.

Forrest had started out the game tight. He had loosened up somewhat as the game progressed, and the money started flowing his way, but as things started to go sideways, he was getting looser and looser. By the time his chip stack was gone, he was playing nearly every hand and getting knocked off over and over. Of course, he never had a chance, but the way he was playing, he couldn't have won even if the game were honest.

There is a phrase in poker language for when a player loses his composure during a bad session. It's called "going on tilt." Forrest was most definitely on tilt.

The game itself had become quieter, more somber as Forrest's fortunes turned. There were no more jokes by the time he reached for his wallet the first time for another five hundred dollar buy-in. It was a fast two hands that cost him the next five hundred and three hands for yet another. And then a series of three hands in a row that he went all in with the five hundred dollars . . . and lost.

Brian had said almost nothing in the first three hours of the game. He had not even introduced himself to Forrest. He just played the game and offered a stray, brief comment here and there. When Forrest reached the point where he had run out of cash, Brian had intended to offer him credit.

Turns out he didn't need to. Forrest asked. Forrest knew it was Brian's game and offered to settle up at the end with a check that he assured everyone was good. I almost felt bad for him. As high as he was just a couple of short hours ago, he was now chastened and beaten down by what he thought was just plain bad luck.

Brian was gracious and said that a settle-up check at the end would be fine, even wished him luck, saying that he hoped he wouldn't need it. He also reminded Forrest that the game would end in ninety minutes as it always did, rain or shine. That was etched in stone, win or lose. Forrest meekly agreed.

The group eased off Forrest at this point, having already accomplished their goal. The game leveled off at this stage, and Forrest won a couple of decent-sized pots, and thus his mood had leveled off as well. As the game moved closer and closer to its end, it looked more like a regular, friendly game of poker.

Forrest won a nice-sized pot and tipped Kirk generously once again, using it as a way to engage Kirk in conversation.

"Where did you learn to deal?" he asked. "No offense, but I haven't seen any Black dealers at The Hope. I was just wondering."

"No offense taken, sir. I work here as my day job, and these guys taught me how to deal. I was actually thinking about applying at The Hope. What do you think, guys? Am I ready?"

Everyone at the table nodded or spoke their agreement that Kirk was indeed ready to become a more formal poker dealer.

Slick added, "You'd probably be better if you dealt me a fuckin' winner every once in a while."

Brian used this as an unplanned opportunity to dig a little further into Forrest.

He said, "I think maybe people have gotten a little too sensitive and woke when it comes to this racist shit. Kirk didn't seem to mind your question, but a bunch of people out there would have found some sand in their pussies over a simple, polite question like that." Brian looked squarely at Forrest as he spoke, clearly implying he wouldn't mind hearing his thoughts on the matter.

"I have actually given this a lot of thought," said Forrest, "and I think that a lot of people of all kinds have gotten a little overly sensitive. I guess that it makes sense in the context of how bad things were and how far we've come, but I can't help but wonder if we are actually empowering racists when we go so apeshit every time some racist dipshit says something stupid.

Think about it. If we just shrugged it off, we would be stripping them of their power and what I think they want most —attention."

The game had actually paused for a moment since everyone had stopped to listen to Forrest. If you have ever played poker, you would know how unusual this is. Most poker games continue, no matter what. Nothing short of a nuclear detonation would interrupt most poker games. It is said that they were still playing poker on the Titanic as it sank.

Forrest continued. "I can't help but think that if we just treated these people as the minor idiotic annoyances they are, we would all be better off. Think of them like the idiot talking too loud in a movie theater or some jerkoff riding a loud motorcycle instead of seeing them as some arch criminal requiring our attention. That would rob them of their power rather than what we do now, which empowers them and gives them what they want most, attention. It's their knowing they have the power to harm and garner attention."

No one spoke for a moment, but Kirk resumed dealing.

"Man," said Alex, "you sure got a perty mouth, but you know what? I think you're right. For the most part, these people are morons and can't ever get anyone to pay attention to them for anything they have actually accomplished, so it's easier to just say daffy shit and then play the victim when they get called out for their stupidity."

The rest of the game went by rather uneventfully. Forrest did manage to mount something of a comeback but not nearly enough to get all his money back. And when it was 5:55, Kirk declared to the players that it was time for the last three hands.

Forrest did not object and seemed resigned to accept the losing situation though it was somewhat less disastrous than it had been at one time. He was down everything he had come with, which I had lost track of but was probably about thirty-five hundred dollars. And after everything was tallied up and cashed in, he still owed Brian a little over thirteen hundred.

The time had come to write the promised check. Forrest reached for his back pocket and pulled out a checkbook.

Sid looked over, squinting just a bit and acting is if he had never seen a checkbook before. "What is that," he asked, "a check? I didn't even know they still existed. Maybe you found a couple in the glove box of your Studebaker on the way over. Hey, I have a quill pen somewhere if you need it to fill out the check."

Forrest grinned and started writing out the check to Brian. "If I were you, I probably wouldn't even cash this thing. My autograph alone will probably end up being worth more."

"To whom exactly?" Brian asked as he looked down at the checks Forrest had handed him.

Brian paused for a moment as he looked at the check and said, "You know, I think I might keep this check, especially since it's not even made out to me. Maybe you should give me another one that has my actual name on it so I can actually cash it."

Forrest was ready with his reply. "Oh, but it is made out to you, sir, but that's okay. I'll give you another one made out to this Brian Louis person. After all, being a government employee as you are, you probably could use the money. I'll tell you what. I'll give you one to cash and another as a souvenir."

The sarcasm thickened with each word Forrest spoke, but if Brian was flustered or intimidated, he most certainly didn't show it and simply accepted both checks, folded them neatly, and put them in his back pocket.

Annie and the men milled about, the winners gloating and the losers ruminating about their bad luck hands and how Kirk, the dealer, was to blame—typical poker game behavior.

Forrest kept his eyes glued on Brian as he said his goodbyes and thanks to each of the players. He made it a point to thank Kirk.

"I don't make a habit of blaming the dealer for my own bad play, and I think you would make a fine addition to any poker room."

Kirk, in turn, thanked Forrest for the generous tips and said he looked forward to dealing to him again in the future, a future that Forrest knew was very much in doubt. Forrest said the rest of his goodbyes, and just like that, he was gone.

16

THE POST GAME SHOW

Nothing much was said among the players ever since Brian had made a shushing gesture, bringing his finger to his lips. It had been a warning to make sure there was no chance that Forrest was still within earshot. Brian walked to the window that had a view of the parking area. It wasn't until he saw Forrest get into his car and drive away that he was ready to talk to the others, all of whom remained in his apartment.

Brian, like the others, had put on a good show for Forrest, but now he seemed worried and troubled as he asked everyone to take a seat. Noticing this, Alex asked, "What the fuck is going on? Why are there two checks?"

As Brian reached into his pocket, removing and unfolding the checks, he answered, "This."

He showed Alex and the others the checks.

"Brian Litvinov?" asked Sid. "Who the fuck is Brian Litvinov, and what is this shit about you being with the government?"

. . .

"I," Brian answered, "am Brian Litvinov. And you need to mind your own fuckin' business."

Except for Ray, the others were bewildered and curious. There was the realization that what they thought they knew and what they actually knew were now two entirely different things.

"I have worked for the feds on and off for most of my life. Forrest's knowing that is not a big deal, but the fact that he's not worried about revealing it to me means that we are in big fucking trouble. Either he doesn't think there is any way we can stop him, or worse, whatever his plans may be are already complete."

"If that's the case, what do we do now?" Ray asked.

"Let's put a bullet in him," said Sid. "I'm an old man. I'll do it. I don't have much to lose. I might as well do something worthwhile with my life."

It meant a lot that not a single person in the room seemed shocked by Sid's suggestion. If you had a chance to go back in time to 1930 and kill Hitler, would you do it? I think most people would. Even though none of us at the time knew exactly what Forrest was planning, we knew enough to know that whatever he was doing was on par with the crimes of Hitler—and conceivably even worse.

"Not a bad idea," said Brian, "but at this point, I doubt it would stop whatever is coming. We need to know more, and there is no time to waste. Thank you for your help, guys, but I need to talk to Ray, Annie, and Tiger alone."

Kirk had just finished resetting and brushing the table, getting it ready for the next game. Ray was cashing out his tips for him as everyone else said their goodbyes. Kirk, of course, knew of the "Black flu" but didn't know much else. As he took his money and prepared to leave, he searched Brian's face for clues.

"Brian," he said, "I don't know what's going on, but I want

you to know that I trust you, and if there is anything I can do to help, all you need do is ask."

"Thanks, kid. You did a great job today. Let's hope we are not too late."

Once the room was cleared, only Brian, Ray, Annie, and I remained.

Brian turned to me and asked, "Tiger, I don't know you that well, but you seem like a pretty straight-up guy. Do you have any particular problem with breaking and entering? Even though it's tribal property, it would still technically be considered a crime."

It's worth noting that he didn't seem to feel any need to ask the same question of Annie and Ray. Ray, of course is his son, and Annie, as far as I can tell, is Ray's girlfriend. I guess he just assumed that they would be up for whatever was asked of them. As usual with Brian, he was right.

"I don't see much choice at this point. What have you got in mind?" I asked.

"I'm not going to get into what I know and how I know it, but if I'm right, what's going on here could make the Holocaust seem like a Sunday brunch.

"Forrest called me out for who I am, Brian Litvinov. The fact that he has access to that level of intel is scary enough. The fact that he wasn't afraid to let me know that he knows who I am is nothing short of terrifying. That means he is so far along that he doesn't think there is anything we can do to stop him."

Ray and Annie sat next to each other on the couch, and as Brian spoke, I saw Ray reach for Annie's hand, gripping it tightly, but they remained focused on his every word, as did I.

"We need to get in there tonight. We can no longer afford to wait for the CDC and DOD even though I know they're on their way. So here's the deal. Don't ask me how, but I used my connections to get you in. There's a shift change at four-thirty this morning. At that point, there will be no guard at the door that connects the two labs from the inside. The three of you should have no problem getting in. Not all of their staff is on board, so you will probably have to dodge some of the other guards.

"Tiger, bring every official tribal document that you can throw into a backpack. If you are stopped, just throw as much weight around as you can. Tell them it is tribal land, and you have every right to be there any time you want. That will at least buy you some time. The one wild card is Forrest. No doubt he knows we are on to him, and I think we know enough about him now to know that he is capable of anything. And he may very well know we are coming.

"Don't ask how, but I got you complete access to their computer systems."

He reached into his pocket and produced a small, innocent-looking thumb drive.

"Insert this into any USB port on any computer in the building, and you will have everything you need.

"Annie, I'm going to assume that you will know exactly what you are seeing."

She nodded.

"Copy everything you can onto this device."

Annie tilted her head, a questioning look on her face. She didn't need to wait long for the answer.

"Yes, I want you to copy all the data. If Forrest is successful, then we are going to need that information to try to find a treatment or cure. This is no ordinary thumb drive. The data will transfer incredibly quickly, three to five minutes at the most. Once the data is on the device, I need you to immediately insert it into your phone. Then dial this number." He handed each of us a small piece of paper with a phone number on it.

Ray looked at the paper and said, "This is real high-tech spy stuff, Dad, a piece of paper with a phone number on it."

He was trying to be funny, but Brian wasn't in the mood for laughs.

"Ray, no joke," Brian said. "I gave one to each of you to make sure that it's not lost, so Annie, immediately plug it in to your phone and just dial this number. Don't do anything else. When you plug it in, it will light up red. When it's done transferring the data, the light will turn green. That's it. We will have everything on his database, and it should take no more than five minutes. Once you are done copying the data, I want you to delete and destroy everything you can on their system.

"My gut tells me that his plan is already in motion, but if it's not, then the loss of his data may set him back and buy us more time, but consider that part a luxury. If you have the time, then great. Go ahead and wipe out his data, but the crucial part is copying and transmitting the data as quickly as you can, preferably without getting dead."

The three of us had been listening to Brian as if our lives depended on it because let's face it, they probably did. Brian was all business, and for the first time, it seemed completely credible to me that this man was not just some spry old man in a nursing home of sorts. This man was a spy and no doubt a good one.

No one spoke for a minute or two. We all seemed to need a breather, a little time to absorb what we were hearing.

Brian continued. "The key to this entire operation is time. Annie will need as much as fifteen minutes to complete her job, hopefully less depending on the wireless connection"

Ray looked up at his father. "So what are Tiger and I supposed to do? What are we even there for?"

"You and Tiger are there as a distraction to buy Annie the time we need, and Annie, you are going straight to a computer and get to work immediately. Ray, you will stay fairly close to Annie but not too close. And Tiger, you will basically wander around until a guard catches up with you. At that point, you're going to throw around as much weight as you can. Keep throwing documents in his face, saying you have every right to be there for an inspection any time you want. Be the biggest asshole you can be. I suspect it won't be that easy for you because you are a pretty nice guy, but you can do it. Just try to channel being a douchebag—we all have one."

I laughed when he said that. "Oh, don't worry, Brian. I'm perfectly capable of being a dick. Just ask any of my exes."

Ray piped up then. "While we're there, why don't we just burn the fuckin' place down, preferably with Forrest in it."

Brian laughed at the suggestion. "Ray, I assume you're serious because you really are my son, but no, there's a chance that innocent people could get hurt, and it really won't do us any good anyway. The whole game here is time. Time is all that matters. Buy Annie enough time to transmit the data and once that is done, just get the fuck out of there."

"And what about Forrest?" asked Ray. "What happens if we run into him?"

Brian paused for a moment, clearly looking for the right words for what he was about to say.

"Guys, I'm not sure quite how to say this so I'm gonna just say it. If you see Forrest in that lab, there is a better than fifty-fifty chance he will simply kill you where you stand. Even if Forrest is not there it's still an incredibly dangerous mission. So I have to ask you, do you really want to do this? I know in my heart that what we are trying to prevent could be the most horrible crime in the history of humanity. And not to make a joke of this but that's a pretty high bar. Humans have done some incredibly horrifying things to each other. If I'm right, and I think you know that I am, this will make most of the other genocides in human history look like a clambake by comparison. But even with all of that said I would not look down on any of you if you refused to go, not even you Ray. There is a very real chance you will lose your lives."

Again, a brief silence settled as the enormity of the responsibility sank into each of us.

"I'm in," I said and looked over to see both Annie and Ray nodding in agreement. "As Sid said, 'If I gotta die, it might as well be for something worthwhile.'"

Brian nodded and said, "I would go with you, but I'm an old man, and I would just slow us down. Besides, this shit is dangerous. I don't wanna die. Fuck that!"

We couldn't help but laugh, shattering the somber feelings of the task at hand.

"Okay," Brian said, "you've got about nine hours 'til go time. I would suggest trying to get a little sleep, but I'm not stupid, so I know that won't be easy. But no sleeping pills or any shit like that. You're going to need to be your sharpest, and pills have residual effects.

"Ray, I figure you and Annie will be together, so just go to our house. Tiger, I need you to pick them up in your car at about four-fifteen. Your window to get into the lab is exactly four thirty a.m., so I don't want you there too early sitting around in the parking lot. Annie, your credentials will obviously get you into your side. Do you think you'll have any problem bringing these two in?"

"No. I know all those guys, and Tiger's paperwork should smooth things out if there's any problem, so no, I think we are good."

"Okay, then," Brian said. "In my line of work, what we just did would be called a mission briefing. Congratulations, you are all now spies or whatever the fuck you want to call yourselves.

"Are we all good? Anybody have any questions?"

No one spoke before Ray finally asked, "Yeah, Dad, I have a question. What's our name again?"

"It's Litvinov, fuckface, and you might as well forget it. That name never did anybody any good."

"Well, maybe it will now, Pop. Maybe it will do a lot of good." Ray had been joking around, but now he was dead serious.

IF BRIAN WAS TOUCHED by the sentiment, I certainly couldn't tell.

"All right, then. Get out of here and go save the world or some fuckin' thing. I have planned a very busy evening of annoying the staff, and I'm actually hungry, but of course, I missed dinnertime again."

"Just order a pizza again, Dad," Ray said as we all headed for the door.

17

HEART AND SOLE

Annie and I were going to do what my dad suggested, which was to go to our house to kill some time until the mission, but Annie wanted to stop by her place first to pick up a few things including a change of clothes.

"What does one wear on a spy mission?" she wondered aloud. "I'm pretty sure they don't cover that in any of the fashion magazines. I hear bright colors are the latest trend in assassin wear this spring."

I laughed and said, "You see? This is exactly why I love you. That and . . . "

"Really?" She interrupted me with a thick, sarcastic tone. "You love me . . . really? That's news to me. I mean it sounds great and all, but when exactly did *that* happen?"

I was a bit alarmed in that kind of way where you know you just fucked up, but you're not really sure what you did.

"I love you, Annie, and not just because you're funny," I said, firm in my conviction that I had fixed whatever it was I had broken. It didn't work quite as well as I had hoped.

"Well, I love you, too, you dumb fuck, but you know, that's the first time you ever told me you loved me. And you said it in a way that you might tell a waiter that your fish is undercooked. Um, excuse me, but it's really a little too raw in the middle, and by the way, I love you.

"You know something? You really are your father's son, and most of the time, that's a good thing, a very good thing, in fact, but not at this particular moment. Your dad is an amazing guy. He continues to get even more amazing the better I get to know him, but with that said, he's not real big on expressing his feelings or emotions. He has an obvious tendency to be exceptionally sarcastic and funny whenever he finds himself drifting towards expressions of emotion or affection. I don't know if that's a trauma response or fear of rejection or ridicule if he shows his true feelings or what, but Ray, does that remind you of anyone?"

I had listened patiently, even dutifully, as I tried to figure out a way to explain both my father and myself. How does a husband live with the loss of his wife, the only love of his life? How does a man grow up motherless with a father so deeply and permanently wounded? I make no excuses for me or my dad. We are as imperfect as anyone else in an imperfect world, but our aversion to expressing feelings makes sense. It makes perfect sense to raise a shield; It makes perfect sense to withhold emotion and affection for fear of pain and loss.

I wanted to say all of this to Annie. By now, we had arrived at her apartment, and she sat staring at me, now with only sympathy, as if she could somehow sense the struggle as I searched for the right words.

I wish I could say that I had told her all that I was feeling, but what actually came out was pure Brian Louis.

"Hey, I don't remember you ever telling me you love me either . . . and by the way, that fish *was* undercooked."

Annie, to her eternal credit, just shook her head and opened the car door, starting toward her apartment. I quickly followed.

There was mostly silence as we gathered the things she needed, but it was not a tense silence. She was clearly sympathetic, but I was under no illusion that this conversation was anywhere near over.

"Here," she said as she tossed me a bottle of water from the fridge to where I was standing in her dining room. "I've got everything I need. Let's get out of here."

We were back in the car and driving toward my place when she said, "So tell me, dipshit, when have you ever heard of a woman saying 'I love you' first, especially a Black woman? And you know god damn well that I love you, and I know you love me."

There was not a hint of anger in her voice as she continued.

"If for no either reason than this . . . we can talk, we can reason, and we can even argue without the slightest chance or thought that we would ever actually try to hurt each other. You don't *need* to tell me you love me because I know it. I feel it in your actions. I see it in your eyes . . . But you know what? As dumb as it may sound, I really do want to hear it sometimes, and I bet if you were being honest with your own emotionally stunted self, you do too!"

By that time, we had made it back to my house and were parked in the driveway. For once I didn't have to think too long about what she said because it was so obviously true. I had no reason or desire to hide from it. Looking back, I wonder what my father might have done in that moment. Would Annie have said enough to break down his carefully constructed wall, or would he have found a way to deflect, making some kind of joke out of it? In that moment, I chose her . . . fully.

"Of course I love you," I said, "and I do love hearing it too. And I will make you this promise right now and forever: I will tell you I love you every single time that I really mean it . . . and that's going to be a lot. It's going to be so much that I hope you don't get sick of hearing it!"

"No, baby. I will never get tired of hearing those words coming from those lips," she said as she brought her hand up to my chin, gently turning me to face her. "And I love you," she said as we both leaned in. Our lips met and our tongues danced as I brought my hands to both sides of her neck and pulled her even closer.

Her hands moved first to my hair and then down to my chest as we stayed locked together in a kiss that felt much like our first. She reached down for my belt, and my breathing sped up as my hands moved to her breasts. I felt her arch her back ever so slightly as our eyes met. Almost as one mind, we broke our embrace and practically jumped from the car. We left all our belongings behind as we made our way with purpose to the front door.

There was a trail of shoes and clothes as we made our way through the house. By the time we reached the bedroom, only our underwear remained, her panties still on but her bra a not-so-distant memory. She lay back on the bed, legs spread only slightly as I removed the last of my clothes. I climbed on the bed between her spread legs and paused just long enough to reflect on what a lucky man I was to have such beauty laid out before me, but more than that, a woman who loves me, who needs me in mind, spirit, and body.

"Kiss me," she said.

I knew exactly what that implied. She was already pulling on one side of her panties as I pulled on the other, and together we left her bare, totally open to me. There was no more waiting, no need for impatience as I brought my lips to her, first very softly, almost teasingly.

I could taste her upon my tongue as I explored all of her. Her legs wrapped around my shoulders, her feet resting on my back. I stopped for a moment, only to catch my breath, and she responded by not so gently putting both hands through my hair, pulling me back to what was now the center of my world.

Soft moans came from her lips as her back arched and her legs stretched across my back.

I would have happily stayed right there forever, my hands exploring wherever I could reach, my mouth bringing her pleasure as I tasted that which flowed from her. She gently pulled my hair, cupped my chin now soaked with her juices, and said one simple word: "Now."

It was not a request.

I reached for the nightstand drawer where I kept condoms for these occasions. As I was about to grab one, I noticed just how many we had gone through and how few were left. Before I removed one, she reached out toward the drawer and gently closed it, looking directly into my eyes.

"Are you sure?" I asked.

"Yes," she breathed, "very."

It was not something we had ever discussed, but in the moment, it seemed completely settled, completely right.

I entered her slowly, teasingly. But I knew her well enough to know that she would take only so much of that. She thrust her hips upwards, engulfing me, pulling me fully inside.

I began a slow rhythm. When the time was right, I paused but just for a moment. Still fully inside her, I pulled away slightly from her hips and moved my body slightly forward and up. I held that position for a moment, staring into her eyes before pulling myself almost completely from her and then quickly back again and forward.

I felt her breath on my face as I brought our bodies fully together, my mouth hungrily upon hers, then moving on to her neck and ear. It was all I could do not to come. I had no choice but to slow my movements, bringing myself back from the edge again and again.

Ann knew exactly where I was and knew she could take me over the edge whenever she chose. And now she did, thrusting her hips and arching her back again and again until the choice was no longer mine to make.

If I had thoughts of pulling out, I cannot recall, but that choice was not mine to make either as she wrapped her legs around my back, her arms around my neck, and held me firmly in place on top of her. It was all hers—as was I—and she mine. We remained locked together, both breathing heavily.

As our breathing slowed, and her grip on me loosened, I rolled over next to her onto on my back and looked over at her. She was crying.

I'm no ladies' man, but I have been with my fair share of women, and I have never seen a woman cry after making love, or just plain having sex, for that matter. I have always had a pretty decent sense of confidence sexually. Whether that is warranted or not, I will never know. I have never asked a partner if she had an orgasm because I realize that no matter what the answer is, it would be meaningless. If a woman enjoys you sexually, she will return to you sexually. It's as simple as that.

I ALSO MIGHT BE unusual in that I've never been particularly concerned about my size. For what it's worth, I think I'm pretty average, but even if I'm not, there isn't a whole lot I can do about it. I have to admit, however, to what I now understand is a totally racist curiosity about the size of the men Ann had been with in her past.

She had told me that I was only her second white partner, and I in turn had told her that she was my first Black woman. She always seemed amused by my indifference to the concept of us as an interracial couple.

I can say in all honesty that it makes absolutely no difference to me whatsoever. I'm not attracted to Black women. I'm not attracted to white women. I am simply attracted to women.

Period. In fact, I've always chuckled when I have heard a gay person being questioned with "When did you know you were gay?" Just once, I would love to hear the person answer, "I don't know, dipshit. When did you know you were straight?" I guess what I'm trying to say is you like who you like, and for me race has no bearing either way. Apparently Ann is much the same way.

But in the here and now, she was crying, and I needed to know why. Of course, my first reaction was to think I had, pardon the pun, fucked up.

"Baby," I asked, "what's wrong?" I leaned in close and stroked her cheek with the back of my hand.

"They want to kill us," she cried, "all of us!"

She was sobbing, and there was nothing I could or should do to stop it.

"Why? Why?" But it was not a question. "How can someone be so smart yet hate so much?"

This was an impossible question, and I made no attempt to answer.

"You know, I must be an idiot," she said, still teary. "I always thought that knowledge was an antidote to hate, but no, of course it isn't. Being smart is just a way to be even better at hate. This piece of shit is trying to kill every fucking one of us, and you know what? He just might pull it off! As a matter of fact, he probably already has! And you know what else? Nobody gives a shit because he's only gonna kill niggers. Hey, they're animals anyway, so let them lose their souls!"

Only then did I finally interrupt her because at that moment, I finally understood what was going on inside her beautiful, distraught mind. I already knew it was significant, or why else would we be sitting here waiting to break into a laboratory in the middle of the night? However, it wasn't until that very moment that I actually *felt* the enormity of it.

"Honey, I'm not going to sit here and say I understand

because I can't. I was born with every conceivable advantage, but what do you mean by 'let them lose their souls'?"

"It was from *The Godfather*. I never saw the whole movie, but when I was a little girl, my father was watching it on TV, and there was a scene where the mob bosses had a meeting about going into the drug business. One of the bosses says, 'I want it kept only in the colored neighborhoods.' He says it just like that. 'They are animals anyway, so let them lose their souls.' Somehow, those words have stuck in my head. Whether I like it or not, that is how I experience my own Blackness . . . that whites will always think of us as animals even when they won't say it out loud."

How could I know? How could I understand? There was simply no way, and I was not going to pretend there was. All I could offer her were my words.

"We care, honey. You, me, and a lot of other people we will never even know. And we *are* going to do something about it."

I could practically feel her wave me off as if those words meant nothing. She doubtlessly wasn't off by much. While those words didn't quite mean nothing, they sure as shit couldn't mean a whole lot.

"You know, when I was a kid, I wrote a short story," she said. I called it 'A Tale of Two Negroes.' It came from a story my grandfather told me. He had a very good childhood friend named Fred Hampton. Hampton became a prominent Black liberation leader and staunch anti-fascist at a very young age.

"My grandfather was sympathetic but wanted nothing to do with the movement. In his mind, it could lead to nothing but trouble. My grandfather was no fool, but he believed that we could succeed by playing by the rules and working hard despite the built-in disadvantages. I think he tried to fool himself into thinking that we had any kind of fair chance. The murder of his friend Fred at twenty-one years old by FBI assassins did nothing to change his mind.

. . .

"MY STORY of the two of them featured Hampton as the fallen hero, a martyr, and my own grandfather as a stooge, a willing slave to a system that treated him exactly as that soulless animal, someone who never even deserved a chance.

"I never showed that story to anyone, and I loved my grandfather, but I never quite got over seeing him as some hapless house nigger going through life saying 'Yes, suh! Yes, suh!' to every white man he met.

"In a way, I hated him for that, yet without that man pushing a broom for almost forty years, I wouldn't be where I am today—brave, proud, and with many of the opportunities that white people have always been able to take for granted. I stand on his shoulders and millions more like him. I still hate that slave mentality, that bowed head, that broken spirit. Moreover, I also stand on the shoulders of people like Fred Hampton, Bobby Seale, Malcolm X, and Assata Shakur, people who set the example of breathtaking bravery and tireless devotion to the cause.

"Still, I struggle with feeling shame for people like my grandfather, the janitors and busboys and servants of a society that still treats them as invisible slaves. Yet in a way, they are heroes in their own right. They are the millions who toil away lifetimes in silence to survive and maybe make something just a little better for their families. They deserve better, and now they face the possibility of being virtually blinked out of existence."

Ann had stopped crying some time ago. We lay side by side, physically and spiritually utterly naked. Finally, at that moment at least, I felt that I understood, that I now had some idea of what it means to be Black in America. No, I knew I was still looking in from the outside, but I think I understood as well as any white man could.

I also thankfully understood that this was an excellent time to just keep my mouth shut and not try to offer some glib cliché or joke. She had bared her soul. I knew as much as anyone just how hard that is. How vulnerable it leaves you. So I was happy just to lie beside the woman I loved, even more so for knowing what I now knew. It wasn't long before I realized she had fallen into a peaceful sleep. I watched her tranquil form, far from the fire of just minutes ago. It wasn't long before I, too, succumbed to sleep.

18

TAKEOUT AND BREAK-IN

It felt like five minutes, but it was almost midnight when I felt Ray gently shake me awake.

"Good morning, my love," he said even though it was far from morning. "You okay, baby?" he asked. "As far as I can recall, I can't remember ever fucking somebody to tears."

He laughed that laugh that makes me want to kiss him and then punch him in the face.

"I'm fine, love, but I'm really hungry, and by the way, don't give yourself too much credit. You didn't actually fuck me to tears. It was more like I was just trying not to laugh at your sorry ass," I said with a smile.

"Yeah, me too," he said. "I could actually eat. I could order some Chinese if you want. I think Spring Garden still delivers this late."

"Sounds good," I replied. "Just get me the usual, and hey, listen. I gotta go take a shower. Somebody—and I'm not saying who—made one heck of a mess down there." She looked pointedly at my crotch.

"Okay, honey. I'll call it in, and you go jump in the shower."

He must have broken some kind of record for ordering Chinese takeout because I was in the shower for literally two minutes when I felt something poking me in the lower back. It was Ray, of course, who had quietly crept into the shower enclosure. As you might expect, I was all wet and soapy, but that didn't stop him from wrapping his arms around me from behind, kissing me on the back and neck. It was as if the fire of a couple of hours ago had not quite gone out.

Despite the soap and water, those embers instantly reignited. I turned my head just enough to find his waiting lips. This might be the corniest thing I have ever thought in my life, but in that moment, my man tasted of love, of the love of my life. He broke our kiss and turned my body, using his right arm to gently lift my leg right above my knee.

This wasn't our first time for shower sex, and I don't care what romance novels might tell you, but the logistics of sex in the shower are tricky at best, but Ray and I had worked out a pretty good method. He lifted my leg and I leaned forward at the waist and grabbed onto the metal bar attached to the tile wall.

I GLANCED behind me to see that he was without a condom. Now it was my turn to ask, "Are you sure about this?" My voice was coy, dripping with soap, water, and sarcasm.

"Yes," he replied, fully aware of the irony, "very! It's not like it matters much at this point," he said, almost laughing.

When we had made love a couple of hours earlier, it had been intense and nearly reverent to the point that I could never imagine feeling closer to another human being than I felt to Ray. Even my orgasm had felt different. The truth is, sex with Ray had never been anything short of great, but our recent union had been at a whole different level, something I could never have even imagined.

However, the truth is that sex in the shower is about two things—having fun and not hurting yourself. We did both.

He entered in a swift, no-nonsense way with a single thrust. From my position, there isn't a whole lot I can do to help him. So I did something that is usually very hard for me to do: I simply closed my eyes and enjoyed it. I felt myself nearing my climax again and purposely held it off. I don't usually do that, but this time, I wanted to wait for him.

I didn't have to wait long. He groaned and clutched me around the waist as he erupted inside of me, and I felt the sweetness of my own orgasm rush through me at that precise moment. We stayed locked together for only a moment because now we felt the water raining down on us and the soap in our eyes and covering our bodies, sensations that just moments ago we were oblivious to. We got down to the business of getting clean. After all, one wants to be clean, fresh, and at their best when breaking into a laboratory to try to thwart a madman.

I got out first and dried off while Ray finished up. It's a good thing I did because the notoriously slow Spring Garden was knocking at the front door only moments after I had thrown on a robe.

I made my way to the front door, grabbing some money along the way. We had ordered from them quite a bit, so I wasn't surprised that I knew the delivery guy.

"You are hungry late tonight, Dr. Byron," he said. I think he might be the only person I know outside the lab who insists on addressing me as "Doctor."

Ray had emerged from the bedroom in shorts and a t-shirt. "Go get dressed, babe. I'll set everything up."

He did and he had also turned on the TV to some random episode of *Star Trek*. A love of *Star Trek* is something we share. I always loved *Star Trek* for its optimism and its vision of a near-perfect world where everyone shared equally and without racism, made all the better by the sharp contrast with the world in which we lived. Plus, I'm a scientist. I'm supposed to be a nerd. I never quite got why Ray was into it. He certainly wasn't the nerdy type, but it was our go-to when we just wanted to put something on TV that we didn't really need to pay attention to, both of us having seen every episode at least twice.

We were halfway through our meal when Ray said, "Well, I guess I might as well tell you about my mother."

I was a bit surprised. I thought I knew everything there was to know since she had passed when he was only four days old. I said nothing and waited for him to continue.

"Just as my father is not who I thought he was, neither was my mother. She did die when I was four days old but not in the way I had been told."

I gasped when he said, "She was murdered by East German assassins. She was a spy, just like my dad, but apparently, even more so.

"From what I can tell, my dad dealt mostly with data and reports. She did that too, but she was also what they would call a field operative. We would call that a spy, a proper spy. My dad doesn't know the exact reason, but as far as he could tell, it was a rogue assassination by a bitter East German who knew that the Cold War was ending. He also knew he was on the losing side."

I didn't know what to say. He had spoken softly and without emotion, but to me, what he was saying was unimaginable. Just as there was no way Ray could understand my journey or upbringing and the challenges I faced, I knew there was no way I could fully understand what it was to have had no mother, then to learn decades later that neither your mother nor father were what you thought they were.

Brian and Ray were a lot alike in many ways. Neither was brilliant in a conventional sense. Both were almost incredibly perceptive and aware of themselves and their surroundings, and both had a powerful sense of empathy that was not at all apparent on the surface—strange birds to be sure, but I loved them both. Only now did I even begin to understand their journey together in the decades that followed the death of Linda, Brian's true love, Ray's mother.

Ray just continued eating, seeming to neither expect or require any response from me.

"So why now?" I asked. "Why after all these years did he finally tell you? Why did he wait so long?"

"I'm not entirely sure. I think what we are doing now has brought everything back to the surface for him. I also think he realized that he would have to take actions that would most likely expose him for what he is, at the very least to us and most likely beyond."

Ray had been speaking plainly, almost in a matter-of-fact way, but now emotion crept into his voice as he continued.

"There was no real need to tell me about my mother after all this time, so I can't explain that. I can't explain why he waited so long or why he finally told me."

Ray was emotional now—or at least as emotional as I had ever seen him.

"Ray," I said, "it's going to take you some time to sort all this out, and there is no need to rush it. Just let it settle, and you will think about it without even realizing you are thinking about it. Your brain just kind of buzzes along in the background on autopilot, but the awareness is still there all the time, trying to make sense of everything. You will never completely resolve it, but in time you will make some sense of it and make your own kind of peace."

Ray is a superb listener and had indeed been listening intently as I spoke, even nodding in agreement once or twice.

"It's a good thing there is no hurry," he answered, "because we sure as hell don't have time for it right now."

For Ray, this was about as big an emotional event as I was ever going to see, and I'm okay with that. I love this man in a way like no other, and I know he loves me.

I think we stand a chance. It won't be long before we will find out what kind of a world we will stand a chance in.

19

EYES OF THE TIGER

I'm no spy, and I'm certainly no professional detective, but I like to think I bring a little something to the table—although certainly not a poker table. During my first meeting with Forrest on behalf of the tribe, I had requested the lab's visitor logs almost as an afterthought. I had been quickly and emphatically refused.

It was one of the few open conflicts between Forrest and me. I pushed hard on the matter, but he was steadfast in his refusal. The very fact that he so adamantly resisted confirmed to me that the logs had to be important.

I did have options. I reported what I knew to the tribal elders, and they consulted attorneys who said we had every right to the logs and could go to a federal judge and subpoena the documents at any time. The law was clearly on our side. The only documents they could have refused us would be those that they claimed would be a threat to national security, which visitor logs clearly are not. The problem, of course, is time. It would have taken at least a couple of days.

Instead, I took a different, more dogged and yet simple course of action. I observed. I simply parked directly in front of the building, which I have every right to do, and watched everyone who came and went. I took pictures of visitors and recorded every license plate number. I even spoke with a few as they were leaving.

For a restricted laboratory, they had an enormous number of people coming and going, and almost everyone that visited was there only once. I quickly learned who worked and belonged there and who didn't. More than a thousand people had visited in three days. About two-thirds of those were Black. The other third were split pretty evenly between white and Asian. There is no way that the sheer volume of visitors could possibly be considered normal.

By the second day, it was abundantly clear that they were also watching me. I have no special talent for this, but it was plain to see, and there was no doubt in my mind, that they didn't care that I knew they were watching me. I'm pretty sure they even wanted me to know.

It wasn't just at the lab either. Any time I left the grounds, one or sometimes two of their nondescript black SUVs followed me wherever I was going. I took it as a sign of respect, but respect is one thing. Potential danger is quite another. I kept my handgun nearby, holstered but loaded and on the front seat next to me, covered by a towel.

I TOLD Brian what I was doing, and it had freaked him out a bit. I know he was worried for my safety, but I'm sure it was also a big part of what led him to the conclusion that this was a surreally dangerous situation. It was Brian who advised what to do with the information I was gathering.

I followed his advice. I sent all of the photos and license plate numbers to the tribe and to Brian. The tribe had the resources and connections to find out the identities of those who had visited the lab. They were even able to obtain the identity of those who drove rental cars through credit card records. They then used the credit card information and then passport information to find out exactly what these people were doing and where they were going.

What I didn't find out until much later is that Brian was doing the same thing but probably with resources equal to or greater than what the tribe had. And what they found was nothing short of terrifying. The people who had been visiting the lab had fanned out literally across the globe with a particular concentration of them heading for African, European, and Asian destinations. Most were already on their way or already there.

For a time I had been thinking that the reaction of my allies here in Allset were, in fact, *over*reactions. By the time I had gotten to the poker game with Forrest, I was under no such illusion.

I had informed the tribal elders of all I had found and urged them to use every one of their resources to get government investigators on the ground here as soon as possible, that these events were unfolding on a global level. It was disheartening for me to learn that they understood but had already been using every tool at their disposal. In spite of their efforts, the government presence here was still nothing out of the ordinary.

Like Ann and Ray, I had some time to kill until the mission. I was nervous about what was to come. I'm pretty sure I wouldn't be human if I weren't, but that didn't stop me from getting some sleep.

I returned straight to my room at The Hope. My SUV shadows from Forrest were nowhere to be seen when I left Springview on my way back to the hotel. I can't say I was disappointed, but it was also troubling. *Were they so far along now that they just didn't care what I did?* That was certainly a possibility, but it was also good in one way.

When I got back to my room, I bolted the door with everything there was to bolt it with. Despite my nerves, I had no trouble relaxing. I watched the local news for a while, seeing all kinds of things I already knew. The "Black flu" was now news, at least locally, even though they weren't calling it that yet. There were now a dozen reported deaths. The ICUs were filling up. CDC investigators were on their way to Allset. Well, it's about fuckin' time!

None of that prevented me from drifting off to a much-needed sleep. My alarm was set for 3:30 a.m.

20

MISSION IMPROBABLE

I arrived at Ray's house at exactly 4:15 a.m. as planned and texted them that I was there. Ray and Ann emerged almost immediately. Ray wore simple black trousers and a long sleeve black t-shirt. He carried nothing. Ann was dressed similarly but carried a small purse, which seemed slightly incongruous. It looked like the kind of purse a woman might carry on a night out, requiring only a few personal items.

Well, this was certainly a night out, and certainly the purse contained the device she had received from Brian and the phone she would use to transmit the data. I was wearing black as well, but I also carried a small black satchel, a "man purse" if you will, that contained some tribal documents as well as my handgun. I had considered holstering the weapon but had decided against it.

They both slid into the back seat saying "Good morning" as they entered. I replied in kind as if this were the most ordinary of days, and we were all together for a typical day of work. I stayed parked for just a moment as we discussed the details of what was a pretty simple plan.

Ann assured me she had the device and the phone as well

as her laboratory ID. She had programmed the number into the phone so she was ready to transmit the data as soon as the device received it from their systems. I, in turn, informed them that I carried some official-looking tribal documents. I also let them know that I was armed. Neither seemed surprised.

At this time of day, it was no more than a five to seven minute drive to the lab. It was exactly 4:25 when we parked in what was Ann's actual parking spot immediately adjacent to the front entrance. We walked through the front door of Ann's side of the lab. A single guard sat at a desk that during business hours would have had a receptionist.

"Good morning, Dr. Byron," the guard said. "Kind of early for you, isn't it?" he asked in a friendly manner.

"Yes. These are my guests," she said, offering him no reason for our unusual visit. "This gentleman is a representative of the tribal owners of this property. You may remember Tiger."

He did remember me from a previous visit and did not ask for any identification. He seemed perfectly satisfied and simply said, "Have a good one."

WE CONTINUED past him and down a corridor. The door that connected the two labs was all the way at the back of this building but on the first floor. It was a relatively short walk through a maze of offices and down a corridor.

The actual laboratory space was on the floors above just as it was at nearly every research facility of this type. The connecting door itself was rather non-descript and had only a sign that read "Emergency Exit" above it. There was never a guard stationed on this side, so there was no desk and no other identifying designation.

This was the first moment of truth. Ray reached over and pushed on the metal bar that ran across the length of the door. It opened as easily as any unlocked door would. We walked through and found a guard desk without a guard. As a rule, that door would have been locked and a guard stationed twenty-four seven, but Brian Louis had delivered as promised, and we had easily passed through an open, unguarded door.

I noticed immediately that there was a computer on the guard's desk. Could it really be this easy? Would this computer do? It's as if we all had the same thought at the same time as we each looked at the computer and then at each other. The computer was clearly powered up, its screen glowing blue in the mostly dim lighting of an after-hours office space.

Ann said quietly, "Hold on a second. I know Brian said to spread out, but we might not need to. Maybe we will get lucky."

She explained quickly that on her side of the lab and most research facilities, there was a single network. They just required different passwords and clearance levels to access particular data. She quickly pulled the device out of her purse and plugged it into a USB port that was easily accessible on the front of the computer.

"If this thing is as magical as Brian said, then we might just get everything we need right here."

The three of us stood staring at the screen. The plugged-in device did light up red almost immediately, but the computer so far had done nothing. We sat staring at a blue screen for what felt like an eternity, but in reality was more like fifteen seconds. Even then, nothing much happened, just a single word followed by an ellipsis. "Copying . . ." appeared on the screen, so small that I had to squint to see it. Nothing else on the screen had changed.

We had been standing and staring at the screen and, again seemingly in unison, we looked up at each other and then started looking around. It was as if we remembered all at once that we had broken into what was supposed to be a high-security lab in the middle of the night, a lab whose accumulation of data was currently being copied onto that innocent-looking device.

We had been so absorbed with what we were doing that for a few minutes, we forgot that we were supposed to be these super-secret "spies." *God, we are such amateurs*, I thought to myself as I unzipped my satchel to give me easier access to my weapon should I need it.

The light stayed red. "Copying . . ." stayed on the screen as the seconds went by. It occurred to me that once it had finished, Annie could attach the device to her phone and start working on wiping out Forrest's database while the data transferred. Another option was not to push our luck and leave while the longer process of transferring data over the phone finished up, which would take us out of harm's way.

I didn't have long to reflect on it because at that point, the light on the device turned green. It was done. We had it.

Ann immediately grabbed it and plugged it into her phone. Nothing on the device lit up.

"Don't worry," said Ann.

The phone was already unlocked, and the number Brian had given us was on the screen. I noticed for the first time how unusual the phone number was. It started with a one and had about fourteen digits.

Ann pressed send. There was no ringtone and only silence when it connected on the other end, but at that moment, the device lit up red. Once again, the data was on its way.

Ann smiled and immediately put the phone in her purse and zippered it up, its light still glowing red.

"So what do you say, boys?" asked Ann. "You want to get the hell out of Dodge, or should I take a crack at wiping their system?"

There was not a lot of time for us to think about it.

"Good morning!" said someone heartily from behind us. "I

see that the ever-resourceful Brian Litvinov has somehow dispatched my guard."

We turned around to find Forrest smiling broadly and holding a particularly nasty-looking handgun in his left hand. I have learned throughout my life that every single one of us responds differently to stress and stressful situations, so Ray's reaction didn't surprise me.

"Wow," said Ray, "I didn't know you were left-handed. You can never trust a fuckin' lefty."

Forrest still smiled and looked over at Ray and Ann, who were standing next to each other.

"So you two are a thing, huh?" Forrest said as if he had just noticed it. "She's a little out of your league, isn't she, boy? But I guess you do have your charms, sort of like a poor man's Brad Pitt, like, I mean, very, very poor—a haggard, destitute Brad Pitt although I doubt Brad Pitt would consider that a compliment. A nigger and a Jew. That's some combination."

Ray looked around and then pointed at himself.

"I'm a Jew?" he asked, his tone clearly indicating that he had had no idea.

"I don't know, Mr. Litvinov. Are you?" asked Forrest, his voice dripping with sarcasm. "Maybe you should ask your father—if you live long enough.

"I would very much like it if the three of you would join me for a nice, civilized conversation. Perhaps we can understand each other better, work out our differences in a polite, civilized way."

"Civilized conversation?" I asked. "That might be the whitest, white-man words ever spoken. No offense, Ray," I said, glancing over at him.

"None taken. We are not all racist pieces of shit like him," he responded.

If Forrest was affected at all by Ray's remark, he certainly didn't show it.

Turning back to Forrest, I added, "A civilized conversation at gunpoint? Even you have to understand what a ridiculous joke that is."

"Nevertheless, I must insist," said Forrest motioning with the weapon. "Join me in my office."

Clearly it was more than a request.

21

BOND VILLAIN FORREST

Forrest could not have had any idea that I had copied the data from his computers. Even if he had been watching on surveillance cameras, there wouldn't have been much to see, and I seriously doubt that he knew because he made no mention of the device or phone I carried in my purse as he walked behind us.

He guided us through a maze of hallways and work areas until we reached his office. I was troubled by his confidence. His demeanor was that of a man whose work was done. All that remained for him was to tie up a couple of loose ends—in this case, us.

As we entered his office, he guided us to three seats that had been arranged in a semicircle facing a fairly small but impressive-looking desk. The office itself was unremarkable, no brass, polished silver, or mahogany, just three comfortable, round, fabric office chairs, the desk, and a pretty ordinary-looking executive chair behind it.

The walls were an institutional beige and held no artwork or design to break up the monotony. It was certainly not an office worthy of a supervillain or a super-anything for that matter, but there we sat.

I was in the center with Tiger to my right and Ray to my left. Once we were seated, Forrest walked around the desk and sat down. After looking around for a moment, he put the gun down on his desk.

"There," Forrest said. "Isn't this nice?"

Our complete lack of response might have told him that no, we didn't think this was particularly nice.

"But it really is kind of funny when you think about it," he said. "I mean, you guys are okay, I guess, but that Litvinov fellow"—he seemed to ponder for a moment—"well, let's just say that he is quite something. However, the idea that you assholes are the best that civilization could muster up to try to stop either the greatest hero or greatest villain, depending on your point of view . . . It's just mind boggling. I mean, I'm not really sure what I was expecting, but I sure thought the world would put up a better fight than this," he said with a gesture towards the three of us sitting silently in front of him.

"But I guess it makes perfect sense," he said, gloating and confident, "because the one thing history has shown us time and time again is that nobody, absolutely nobody, gives a shit about niggers."

He had stared directly and purposefully into my eyes when he said the word. "Hell, even niggers don't care about niggers," he said. Our gazes had now locked together.

I think he was right, by the way. What he had said at the poker game about empowering racists by over-responding to every racist slight, both real and perceived, makes the everyday, redneck jackoff racist feel strong and still in control of his world. But what we are talking about here is a completely different animal. This piece of shit was using that word with a purpose: shock me into impotence and hopelessness. If he were even half as smart as he thought he was, he would know that would never happen.

"So tell me," he continued, "don't you want to know why I did it? Well, wait. I'm getting a bit ahead of myself. First, you need to know exactly what I did. It's really quite ingenious if I do say so myself.

"I didn't create just one virus or even one variant. I created fourteen . . . or was it fifteen variations? Forgive me. I've lost count. It might actually be sixteen variations, all of which have different levels of virulence, contagion capability, and relative deadliness, thereby making it virtually impossible to synthesize an effective antidote. Plus, virtually every version has the capability to mutate, becoming either more or less deadly or contagious and even harder to contain.

"THEY DO SHARE one thing in common though. Every one of them has the ability to kill or sterilize Black people. And again, please forgive me. In my efforts to kill or sterilize every nigger on earth, I hope you understand I had to cast a pretty wide net, genomically speaking.

"On a scientific level, and I'm sure you know this, Miss Annie, it's pretty tricky to define Black. After all, we all share part of the same genome because we all came from the same place and are one species. That means there's going to be a whole, heaping helping of dead spics, chinks, Arabs, and even some white folks that find themselves dead or shooting blanks or otherwise utterly incapable of conceiving.

"This is certainly a case of too many is better than too few. Better to kill or sterilize a few innocent white bystanders than it would be to spare even one nigger. My only regret is we probably won't get all that many Jews, but we should be able to knock off a good chunk of those Sephardic fuckers.

"Oh, and Tiger, please don't feel left out. By the time this is all over, I doubt there will be enough of you red folks left to field a basketball team, let alone build another rip-off casino. So go ahead, feel free to have a drink or two. I know you want one. Some of the earliest genomic experiments revealed the Indian "drunk gene." You get drunk faster and addicted quicker. Well, at least you're a cheap date, even cheaper when you are dead."

"It's not going to work you know, you ridiculous dipshit," Ray said seemingly taking every opportunity to insult Forrest. "Even if you are successful at creating a world of giggling, cheerful white people, do you really think it will end there? They will just figure out some new thing to hate about each other—God, height, weight, eye color, dick width. Who the hell knows? But history shows that we can always find a reason to hate and kill each other."

"Wrong," said Forrest abruptly. "*White European history* teaches that— greed, envy, violence, and a winner-take-all, no-holds-barred fight for every scrap of food, every drop of oil. That's white European history and not necessarily the real human condition. We might just find out that with more space between us and fewer mouths to feed, humanity is not all that bad, even white humanity.

"Now as a sociological experiment, it would have been far more interesting to remove white Europeans from the equation since they're the ones who have been in control and the actual purveyors of hate, violence, and racism for a millennium, long enough that none of us have ever lived in a world where we could know anything different or better. It would be far more interesting to kill all the white folks and then see if the true magnanimous nature of humanity emerges, but then that would kind of defeat the purpose of the whole thing, wouldn't it? Oh well, what are you gonna do? So, so long nigs, but the rest of us are gonna have more than enough room and plenty of resources. A couple of months from now, we can just put up a 'for rent' sign in Africa."

Tiger had been sitting quietly but alertly as Forrest went on his rant, but he had been observing keenly, almost measuring the man and the room in which we sat. Finally he spoke.

"There is a legend among my tribe," said Tiger in a tone of voice clearly intended to confer serious wisdom, "that we carry the sins of this life as stones into the next so as to weigh down our tendency to do evil. For most of us, they are but a handful of pebbles or perhaps a small rock, but you, Forrest, you will carry the weight of mountains upon you into the next life and beyond. I do not hate you. I have no fear of you when by all rights I should, but I pity you. I pity the sickness of your soul."

"Ooh, a parable," said Forrest. "That's great! I love those! What kind of an Indian would you be without some kind of boring folksy fairy tale? Nice! Thanks. I think we all enjoyed it, but here, Tonto, try this nonsense on for size.

"How about the death of every nigger is actually the Christian equivalent of the Black man on the cross, dying for our sins just as Jesus did? Extra bonus fun fact: if there really was a Jesus, he was probably Black or so goddamn close to it that it wouldn't make a difference. So there, I call your stupid parable and raise you an obnoxious proverb. Besides, we have a rich history in this country of blaming the victim. Trust me. By the time this is over, the world will be blaming niggers for being too weak to stop their own genocide."

"Okay," said Ray. "I'll bite. Why are you doing this? What the fuck is so wrong with you that you want to be remembered as the absolute worst person to ever come sliding out of a woman's hole?"

Forrest seemed thrilled, excited that someone had finally asked the question.

"I will answer you," he said, "but first, I want to thank all of you, especially your father," he said, looking at Ray. "Without you imbeciles, I would probably still be putzing around trying to get everything perfect when it really doesn't need to be. You rushed me just enough, and for that, I thank you.

"And the real truth is that if it wasn't me doing this, it would almost certainly have been someone else. The technology exists. Pandora's Box is open, and it's kind of like a gun owned by some redneck or a fighter plane ordered by the U.S. government.

"Human nature, at least white European human nature, demands of us that we actually *use* the tools of destruction that we create. We couldn't wait to drop our shiny new nukes on Hiroshima. We enjoyed it so much, we dropped a second one for no apparent reason that anyone at the time could think of, but we did it anyway just to watch the big *boom, boom* and the bodies fry.

"On a smaller scale, do you think Joe Redneck owns thirty-seven guns because he wants to collect them? Of course not. Most of those ammosexuals are just dying for the opportunity to shoot something, anything. Knowing them, they're probably jerking off their tiny little cocks all over them."

As he was speaking, I kept glancing down at my purse. I couldn't tell if the light had turned green, indicating that the transfer was complete, and we did indeed have his data. I waited for what I thought was a good opportunity and slowly unzipped my purse a little at a time until it was open enough for me to see the glow of the light coming from the device inside. It was green. It was done. We had his data.

"So why did I do this? Why am I in the process of killing every Black person on the planet?"

"Because you are a dickless lunatic with a chip on your shoulder," offered Ray helpfully.

"No, Ray. You should really try to have a little sympathy. It might be good for you. It's a sad story really." Forrest continued undeterred, almost gleefully sarcastic and condescending. "It's so many things, and I have suffered so horribly.

"It could be that Black servant who threw away my favorite toy when I was just a boy, or maybe it was that fat cocked Black guy who dicked down and stole my high school girlfriend and broke my heart. Maybe it was that Black girl in grade school who stabbed me in the ass with a fork shortly after I dumped a bowl of ravioli on her head. I mean, who knows? Maybe it was some schvatza that cut me off in traffic.

"By the way, one of those is actually true. I'll let you guess which one . . ."

Forrest had been speaking sarcastically, almost as if none of that actually mattered. And you know what? It really didn't matter because it was becoming painfully clear to me as he spoke that there was truly only one reason for who he was and what he had done: fear. He was afraid of us. He was afraid of everything. And like most of us, we will do almost anything to avoid fear. I could see through him now. He was just a scared, pathetic little man.

As he continued to speak, he kept looking over at me, and despite my best efforts, he noticed me glance into my purse. He turned his full attention to me and said, "What do you got in there, Moolie? What's in the purse? Give it to me!"

He gestured with his left hand, leaning forward and began to reach for it. At this point I certainly didn't mind giving to him, and as I reached to grab it, I noticed on the screen a simple two word text message from Brian: "Got it!"

Tiger glanced over and, seeing the green light, asked me, "Does that mean what I think it means?"

I just nodded.

Forrest reached forward to grab the phone, and I, in turn, reached forward to hand it to him.

Why not? It no longer mattered. The damage was done. For

the first time, Forrest seemed to notice the device attached to the phone.

"You fuckers got my data, didn't you?" he asked with a growing look of puzzlement on his face.

That was the first time tonight I heard him speak with anything less than supreme confidence. Turns out they were his last words.

The next few moments were a blur. As Forrest reached for the phone with his left hand, Tiger leaned toward the desk and used his own left hand to gently push Forrest's hand. With his right hand, Tiger smoothly picked up the gun off the desk, stood fully, righted his posture, and then for just the tiniest fraction of a moment, stood straight up with the gun pointed squarely at Forrest.

There were two incredibly loud and fast gunshots. The first bullet hit Forrest just under his eye, the second right next to his lip. The front part of his face tore away from the rest of him as his entire body turned and fell partially on the desk before finally slumping onto the floor. He landed face down, fortunately, and most definitely quite dead.

Again, every person responds differently to stress, danger, and now death.

"I just couldn't stand the sound of his fuckin' voice anymore," said Tiger.

He was still standing, gun still raised, but he slowly relaxed and lowered it, almost certainly in shock.

"I WONDER which of his stories was true," I said almost robotically, as if it could possibly matter. But I was stunned and probably in shock myself.

"Fuck him. Who cares?" said Ray, clearly not in shock. "He was a shitty poker player anyway."

22

NOW WHAT?

It was not the first dead body I had ever seen. In my line of work, I've seen more than my fair share of cadavers, but it was the first time I had seen a person shot dead right in front of me. I'm pretty sure Tiger had never seen a dead body before, let alone be the one to actually pull the trigger.

Ray seemed unfazed though not exactly unaffected. My first thought was *what we do now*? It occurred to me to call Brian and let him know that Forrest was dead and try to find out what kind of data we got, but there wasn't a lot of time to consider our next move. The gunshots had attracted three armed guards.

They burst into the room with weapons at ready and immediately relieved Tiger of the gun he now held at his side. Tiger then carefully removed and handed over the handgun he had deposited in his satchel.

Now, we three harmless-looking assassins sat quietly awaiting whatever was next. The three guards stood watch over us until the police arrived. Two uniformed Allset police officers soon found their way to the office that had belonged to the late

Forrest Reagan. Because this was Nonya tribal sovereign land, there was some confusion about what to do with us. Barely anyone spoke to us as we patiently awaited our fate, and we did not even talk to each other although I do recall Ray warmly holding my hand and mouthing an occasional, silent "I love you."

We were there for well over an hour. I couldn't quite see Forrest's dead body from where I was sitting, and I was surprised at how quickly I became not uncomfortable with the idea of sitting several feet from a still-bleeding corpse.

None of the cops or guards were paying us any mind, so I took the opportunity to text Brian. He told me that the data was fully received, and he had already passed it along to the tribe, and several government agencies including the CDC and the FBI. He also sent the information to an isolated cloud drive that only he had access to in case something went wrong or if Forrest's connections ran even deeper than we thought, and the government itself might make some effort to cover it up.

More importantly, the data included everything—everything we would need to fight what was already here and what was surely coming. I had already sensed that when I saw the sudden change in Forrest's demeanor as he realized that we had the data. I felt a certain satisfaction in knowing that he was stripped of his certainty of success in his demented mission just moments before he died, and that was a good thing. Fuck him. Brian said it was likely we would eventually be arrested, and he was already working on getting us out.

Tiger was also using this time productively. He was in contact with the tribe, bringing them up to date on what happened and planning for our release.

Brian was right, and the cops did indeed arrest us. We were handcuffed, read our Miranda rights, and peacefully walked through the building and out the front entrance. I had to stifle an ironic laugh. Officials and military personnel flooded the building and parking lot. I wondered if the scene was the same over on my side of the lab.

Their interest was already long overdue, but here they were. The cavalry had indeed arrived. It was probably a coincidence, but it occurred to me at the time that all we had to do to get some attention was redecorate Forrest's office with his brains.

We were led out into the early morning sunlight. News trucks, reporters, and official-looking vehicles filled the lot, empty just hours ago in the darkness. After a bit of official confusion, we were all seated, still handcuffed, in the back of a white van. Moments later, we were on our way.

As it turns out Allset does not have its own jail. Our destination was the prison of Greene County, New York.

23

FIRST THINGS FIRST

There is something I learned as a schoolboy some six decades ago when, as a child, I felt overwhelmed by school. The work expected of me in first grade was more than any human being could possibly keep track of, let alone complete. I can't remember if someone taught me this or if I just worked it out on my own over time, but the lesson is this: anything more complicated than telling time can't be done all at one time. I learned that you can't accomplish more than one thing at one time, and that every task can be broken down into small, manageable steps. This remains true for things as simple as a grocery list and as large as preparing actionable intelligence reports for the President of the United States.

When the data from Forrest's computer came pouring in and only a few minutes later was complete, I took an exceedingly deep breath and began to glance at what we had. I was instantly flooded with that feeling of that first grade boy that I had been, and was still at heart.

Literally, thousands of things needed to be done to minimize the horror of what was unfolding, but the man I had become had learned his lesson: I couldn't do the second thing until I did the first, and the first order of business was to get the kids out of jail and back here. Almost none of the things on this massive to-do list could even begin until that was done.

I knew that Tiger had been in contact with the tribe because their legal counsel had just called me. I was going to try to use some of my connections to get them out, but I also knew the tribe could do it much more easily and cleanly. This crime, if you can really call it one, was committed on tribal land, and they were the only ones with clear legal jurisdiction. Their counsel assured me that they would be released without any pending formal charges by late this afternoon if not sooner. All it would take was a phone call to the New York State Attorney General. Legally there could not even be an official record of the arrest, in case that was a concern to Ray, Tiger, or Ann.

I was not much affected by the fact that Tiger had technically committed a murder. I had no moral issue with it whatsoever. My concern was more practical. Once I knew we had all the data from Forrest's computer, there was no further use for him in terms of what was coming. There was probably not anything he knew that was worthwhile that wasn't already in the files, and I doubt he would have had any kind of "come to Jesus" moment where he suddenly gave up a lifetime of work and demented ideology to try and actually help. He was gone, and that was undoubtedly for the best.

I'm no scientist, so my first few glances at his files didn't reveal much to me except for his intent. There was no doubt that it was his mission to kill or sterilize every Black person in existence. I would never understand the scientific nuts and bolts of how this would happen, but there was no mistaking the objective.

I shifted my attention for a time to the television and social media. Only hours ago, this was a Black flu in a fairly isolated part of upstate New York. Clearly, that was no longer the case.

Seemingly out of nowhere, there were cases of the Black flu all over the world, so much so that the term "Black flu" was already the commonly used phrase to describe the illness and what was happening.

I'm an old man, and most people my age have limited or no understanding of social media. I'm no genius, but because of my work, I had no choice but to stay current, and I was always pretty well connected to social media. It would be fair to say that my interaction with it was more like someone in their thirties than someone in their seventies, that is to say, I understood it. I participated in it. I even mostly enjoyed it, but it was not my lifeblood as it is for most people younger than I am. What was happening now on social media was nothing short of an unprecedented explosion. The phrase "Black flu" was trending pervasively across every platform. News—real, inaccurate, unfounded, or exaggerated—was everywhere.

It was already clear to me that Forrest would have been successful, or damn close to it, if not for the information we now possessed. To stop the spread of this hideous contagion would require nothing short of a massive, worldwide effort sustained over years.

As I awaited the return of Ann, Ray, and Tiger, I was thinking and writing notes. My first thoughts were about what a worldwide response might look like. Can governments, corporations, and political rivals come together to try to minimize the damage—and would they? I was somewhat optimistic that the world would at least try, but how that would play out would only be known over time.

I soon settled in to think about what we could do here and now with the resources already available. The tribe owned the land on which the laboratories sit. They could seize the physical property immediately, and they would soon do just that. The federal government could, and soon would, nationalize

GeneWorks's assets and then dissolve it as a corporate entity. However, what interested me were the people.

This worldwide horror had been created and unleashed from a laboratory almost walking distance from where I sat. It only made sense to me that it should be the center of the efforts to stop it, and there were no better people qualified to cure the disease than the ones who created it, so the question occurred to me whether these scientists knew or not. Did they know what they were working on and why? Ann was probably the most qualified person on the planet to answer that question, but first things first.

I thought that with enough time to look over the files, Ann would be able to know which scientists were complicit, but the more I thought about it, the more I realized that finding collusion could not be the priority. The files contained everything, including every personal e-mail of every employee. This alone presented a huge problem for any number of reasons, including whether or not these people would eventually be prosecuted, but in the here and now, the top priority was to determine whether they were indeed part of the crime and could therefore be part of the solution.

When Ann gets back, the first thing on her to-do list would be to start fighting the virus, hopefully with the help of the people who created it. Figuring out who knew what and when and who was in cahoots with Forrest would have to wait. On some level it didn't matter if they knew what horrors they were producing; they would still be the best hope for treatments, vaccines, and cures. They would have to be a part of the solution, willingly or unwillingly

No matter what, the first order of business in Allset would have to be keeping that laboratory running, but its purpose would now be trying to fix the problems it created. As it turned out, we would have to restore all the data to the laboratory because Forrest had destroyed the lab's data from the afterlife.

Actually, he had programmed the hard drives to reformat and erase everything at 6 a.m. that same day, thereby slamming the barn door right after the horse had escaped. I had already transmitted the data to the tribe and half a dozen government agencies, but a big part of me was wondering if we were now doing the same thing, because this horse was most definitely out of the barn.

My always-unlocked apartment door swung open and there stood Ray, Ann, and Tiger, looking tired and weary but otherwise none the worse for wear. No words were spoken as I hugged each of them in turn. I could see tears in Ann's eyes.

"Okay, guys," I said, "I would love to hear about everything that happened, but it's going to have to wait.

"Tiger, contact the tribe and have them lock down that laboratory. They have all the files, so have them contact every employee to report to work the day after tomorrow. They will be informed of their duties going forward, and they will be paid. The finances can be worked out later.

"Ann, I need you to start going over the data, but the first thing we need are the scientists. Don't worry about trying to figure out if they knew what they were working on. I hate to say it, but ultimately, I don't really care. Like it or not, those motherfuckers are going to start working on a cure under your direction. If they are to be prosecuted later on, we'll have plenty of time to figure that out, but first things first.

"I know it will be hard, but all of you need to get some sleep.

"Ray, I'm coming back with you to the house. Ann, it's probably better if you come with us, but if you want to go to your own home to sleep, that's fine. Tiger, go back to the hotel and sleep, and then come back to my house when you are ready."

. . .

ALL THREE HAD JUST LISTENED as I spoke, and when I was finally finished barking out these commands, it was my son who finally replied.

"Who the fuck died and made you boss?" he asked with a smile.

That's my boy.

"By the way, Dad, not that it matters, but are we Jewish? Forrest told me I was a Jew."

Brian was not surprised by the question and answered it honestly.

"I am not, Ray, but you are—at least technically. Your mother's maiden name was Rosenberg. Her family was extremely devout Orthodox Jews. In the Jewish religion, if your mom is Jewish, then you are Jewish. They never much cared for my disregard of religion, and to be sure, they never much cared for me either. After your mom died, they wanted nothing more to do with us.

"To be honest, Ray, I don't think you missed out on much. Devout, orthodox people of any religion suck. They just do. They do way more harm than good. That's one of the few things I got right, kid. You were way better off without them."

Ray had listened respectfully but had no reply. What a nice Jewish boy.

24

THE HORROR

The six months following the death of Forrest Reagan were a blur of gruesome statistics far beyond the scope of anything in human history— more than eight hundred million dead. Almost three-quarters of the dead were on the African continent. Ninety percent overall were Black. We didn't yet have the estimates of the number of people who had survived but had been rendered sterile due to infection by one or more versions of the virus.

The world had indeed united to fight the virus, but Forrest had been thorough. To be honest, there was nothing he did that was scientifically novel or creative. Virtually all the tools used to create this devastation were readily at hand. It took only his marginal competence, mental illness, and utter amorality to unleash his plague upon the world.

He had been true to his word. There were, in fact, at least sixteen versions of the virus, varying in level of contagiousness and deadliness. Each of the versions of the virus was perfectly capable of mutating into more or less deadly or contagious versions.

When it comes to viruses, there is usually something of a sliding scale. The more deadly the virus, the less contagious it usually is. The reason is simple: dead people can no longer spread the virus. While Forrest was not particularly creative, he was certainly clever and determined. That, I cannot take from him.

All of the various strains of the virus they created would kill anyone with a genome that was susceptible, but most of the strains killed slowly. In many cases, it could take weeks if not months for death to occur.

At this point, scientists were already quite sure that some of the strains might take a year or more to kill the victim. What's more, many of the strains left the victim asymptomatic for weeks or months. Forrest had created the almost perfect balance of deadliness and contagiousness to maximize the spread. Because of this, the world's scientists quickly came to a consensus that preventing the spread was so nearly impossible that it was not worth the resources to even try. Every person of every race could be infected and carry and spread the virus, but obviously not everyone would suffer symptoms of sterility or death, so nearly everyone was infected almost overnight. In fact, by the time a test was developed, less than one percent of the millions who were tested were negative.

As the data came in, it became increasingly clear that this virus had already spread to nearly everyone and would be around for years, so the focus of research became a search for treatment and vaccines. At some point, significant resources were aimed at preventing sterilization and vaccines that would protect both the unborn and the newborn.

Of course, the data we had killed Forrest for was invaluable and the basis of almost all of the efforts to stem the tide. It was

Black people who were the target, but as Forrest had promised, this blade was not particularly precise.

Many millions who did not match the traditional definition of Black were already dead. Among the victims were many of Asian, Arab, and Southern European descent as well as many victims who were white. As that piece of shit had also promised, there was already a multitude of victims among Native American and Inuit populations.

Forrest's tactic for spreading the virus so quickly and widely was again not particularly brilliant or creative, but it was incredibly effective. He had sent out almost two thousand carriers from the laboratory in Allset to all parts of the globe. Again, all it took was the absolute desire to kill and cause harm without reservation.

Most of the carriers had been told they were part of clinical and long-term research that was meant to prevent future pandemics. Internal communications revealed that the carriers were told that they were meant to travel remotely in order to track a theoretical infection pattern that would help scientists in the future be more prepared for outbreaks. It was a perfectly plausible cover, and the carriers had been paid quite well. That combination produced more than enough willing participants who certainly didn't mind a nice payday and free travel.

Of course, it did not work out for them that way. Within days of Forrest's death, we knew enough to begin finding and rounding up the carriers. All but a handful were still alive but of little clinical value. All of the strains were soon known and identified from the data on Forrest's computers.

The carriers themselves were not prosecuted. It was clear that none were willing partners or understood the purpose of their travel. But obviously all were infected and would have to live out whatever remains of their lives knowing that they participated in the worst crime ever committed against humanity. More than three-quarters of the carriers were themselves

Black. I can only imagine the guilt that they must endure. More than a dozen suicides have been reported among the surviving carriers.

Dealing with the investors, financiers, and executives of GeneWorks produced an interesting result, one that Forrest almost certainly would have hated. An international law enforcement arm was created almost overnight. It was created separately from the massive scientific efforts that were now being conducted worldwide but centered in Allset.

This international police and intelligence group was made up of members of every nation but coordinated mostly through the U.S. and China. Its sole purpose was to find and investigate every investor in GeneWorks. Eventually a world court was set up through coordination with the United Nations. Those who had knowledge of GeneWorks's true mission would be fully prosecuted and punished for crimes against humanity. GeneWorks was not a publicly traded company. You couldn't just buy shares on a stock exchange, but in many cases, ownership was blurred by investments from hedge funds and venture capital firms.

The effort to haul investors into court was hardly the point, but it was quite a remarkable side effect. The very act of prosecuting investors and executives for the crimes of a corporation was always notoriously and extremely difficult, certainly in the United States, at least. For example, Lee Iacocca purposely murdered drivers and passengers of the Ford Pinto during the 1970s. The automaker knew the car could easily burst into flames and kill people, yet they made a financial calculation not to use an available cheap and simple fix. Even though this was proven in court, not one Ford executive or investor faced even a single criminal charge.

Forrest changed all of that although I'm quite sure he wouldn't have been happy about it. The legal precedents set in the prosecution of GeneWorks executives and investors would eventually change the world forever. Gone was the notion that a corporation could commit crimes without legal and criminal jeopardy for its individual executives and investors. Proof of their prior knowledge of the crimes was enough to convict them.

FINALLY, don't forget the scientists of GeneWorks who carried out the genocidal details of Forrest's demented vision. There were nearly three hundred of them. A small handful fled Allset and were quickly arrested. It was no coincidence. The files promptly revealed that they had full knowledge of the only real goal of GeneWorks—genocide.

They were jailed and eventually prosecuted and convicted of crimes against humanity. It is important to note that none were executed. In fact, out of hundreds of investors, executives, and scientists that were eventually convicted, only six were ever executed and even then only by orders of the officials of the nations that held them. The executions were a rare display of disunity in the world when dealing with the people and effects of the crime.

The rest of the scientists stayed in Allset and were swiftly put back to work, now looking for cures and treatments for the very same viruses they themselves had created. They were watched and monitored by various scientific and law enforcement agencies as they worked, but work they did.

As the investigation continued, it was clear that many of these scientists would later be prosecuted, and it seemed that many were very enthusiastic about their work in the hope that their contribution to a cure or treatments might mitigate some of their own moral or criminal responsibility for the disease itself.

The fact that the world came together so quickly and so completely to try to cure the viruses would be among the unintended consequences Forrest had created. Of course, corporate responsibility was another.

It could be argued that Forrest had also created a world of genetically improved Black people. Surviving Blacks did indeed end up with extremely efficient and responsive immune systems, traits that were thankfully passed on to their children.

There were now far fewer Black people, to be sure, but without question, they would live on forever despite a madman's efforts and in part because of them.

25

THE RACES

I did, in fact, go back to Ray and Brian's house that morning as Brian had so strongly suggested, and after that day, I never really left. Yes, I kept my apartment for a while and went back there occasionally to pick up a few things, but from that day on, I lived with Ray and Brian.

Brian had moved back to his home and never did return to *Springview*. And I did, in fact, sleep that day although I can't imagine now how I was able to. Of course, I awoke to a very different world.

The very next morning, the true work began. As Brian had suggested, we immediately worked on reassembling the staff from Forrest's side of the laboratory. I was fully aware that there were plenty of guilty among the innocent, plenty of complicit, racist scumbags I was now enlisting in the service of the mission to save lives from what they themselves had created. I knew that in time, the backlash would occur, and the guilty would pay, but for now, all that mattered was the race against time.

. . .

On the second day back to work, I assembled all of the remaining scientists, who were now under my direction. Almost all of them were in attendance. We met in a small lecture hall on the third floor of the laboratory with a fair amount of space, but it was standing room only. I'm not big on public speaking and I kept it short, simple, and to the point.

"Every single one of you in this room bear the responsibility for the horror and devastation we are now witnessing. At the very least, some of you will face prosecution and spend your remaining lifetime as a pariah, the living antithesis of all that is good and just in humanity. That is the least you deserve. All of you in this room either knowingly or unknowingly are part of the worst crime in human history, so I now present you with a simple choice: Stay—and save as many souls as you can, or leave—and sacrifice your own soul. The choice is yours."

At the time, they did not know that the choice was not really theirs. We already had mechanisms in place that would keep them in Allset and keep them coming to work, but the speech gave me a pretty good opportunity to see who was who and what was what, not to mention that seeing what their choice would have been (if they actually had one) would tell me a lot. There was more to the speech, but that was pretty much the gist of it.

I had set up an office for myself on what was Forrest's side of the lab. I could have taken his office but chose not to. Fuck him. Plus, there were still telltale signs of his sick, disgusting brains on the desk and floor.

Later that afternoon, I had something of an answer to the choice I had posed at the meeting with my colleagues. One of the lab's top scientists stopped by my office. He seemed embarrassed as he asked if I had a few minutes to speak with him. Of course, I welcomed him.

He was incredibly nervous as he spoke, and I did all I could to relax him and calm him down if for no other reason than I didn't have much time to waste on conversation.

"I think I knew," he said, "or at the very least, I should have. There were more than enough clues. I ask myself everyday why I did nothing to stop it while there was still time, and I don't like the answer.

"I never thought of myself as a racist, but I don't think anyone ever does . . . except maybe the truly sick fucks."

I thought it was cute that he was embarrassed by his use of a curse word as if this was the worst thing we had to worry about.

He continued. "But some sick part of me must not have minded what he was doing, and for that, I can never be forgiven. Don't get me wrong. I'm not here for absolution. It is not yours to give, nor is it anything I will ever deserve from you or anyone else, but I do ask for one thing.

"I want to be remembered as someone who gave his all to save as many people as I could. I know that someday I will pay for these crimes, but for now, I just want to be as big a part of the solution as you will let me in saving as many lives as I can."

I paused for a moment to consider his words. He was holding back tears as he stared at me. I'm sure he was hoping for some small sign of what I may say next.

"You will be as big a part of saving people as I am. And you are right. No matter what you do from this day forward, I cannot offer you absolution. I doubt that anyone can, but I promise that I will make a full and honest report to any authorities who may ask."

He interrupted. "Please, do not misunderstand. I am not here trying to recruit you for my defense. I do not expect your help in any way. What will happen to me when this is all over will happen. I will face the music. After Man is done with me, God will be my judge, and that I can and must live with."

With that, he stood and uttered a quaint nicety, given the circumstances.

"Have a good day, Doctor Byron."

With those final words, he left.

I kept my office on my side of the lab, too, but I was almost never there. My side had been converted into functioning as a "compile and review" locale for the data coming in from the other side. Obviously our "orphan" work had been suspended, but in yet another unintended consequence of this horrible event, our research conducted in the aftermath of the disaster ended up providing invaluable data for future "orphan drug" research that led to numerous treatments and cures for many of those ailments. It brought me a perverse form of pleasure every time I thought about the good things that had resulted from the hideous acts of Forrest.

More benefits came to light as well. This disaster had led to unprecedented cooperation between many countries with a history of hostility towards each other. Russia had its own long and very secret history of genetic and viral research. Almost immediately, they made that research available to me and others working on treatments and vaccines. The U.S. and China settled into something of a political partnership. The usually politically cautious and standoffish Chinese were incredibly open and generous with all forms of resources.

Israel is a center and source of much of the world's pharmaceutical research and immediately set about focusing all of their efforts on the virus. The disease had inordinately affected much of the Arab world, and the Israelis wasted no time or effort in offering assistance to their former enemies. The bridges of goodwill built during this time of crisis eased and reduced centuries of tension between many historical political rivals, including Israel and Arab nations.

We were now exactly thirty weeks past what I referred to as "dead Forrest day" though I never called it that to anyone but myself. The death toll was now a staggering 1.4 billion with god only knows how many still alive but sterile or awaiting death. Because of the scale of the tragedy and the efforts of the media and Tiger's tribe, the four of us had already attained an unwitting and not at all desired celebrity status. Partially because of that status, some areas of Allset had become off-limits to civilians and especially media.

Part of the reason, of course, was the government's monitoring of the movements and activities of the remaining scientists on what had been Forrest's side of the lab. As much as I'm not a big fan of heavy-handed government actions, it was certainly justifiable, and I'm definitely not complaining.

My days consisted of fourteen hours or more at the laboratory, followed by a meal with Brian and Ray and sometimes Tiger and then as much sleep as I could get before getting up and doing it all over again. I have to admit that the routine brought a certain sense of peace and purpose. I liked the ability to go about my business without interference and many of the day-to-day annoyances of normal life.

My scientists, literally thousands of other scientists around the world, and I were running not just one race but a series of races. The goals of our research had many facets, the first of which was an actual cure. This was the Holy Grail that none of us actually expected to reach, but that research would bear its own fruit even while almost certainly failing to find a single, universal cure.

Research into treatment for the illness had actually shown a great deal of success. In many cases, we had been able to prolong life and even get to the point where people might live relatively normal and long lives. A lot of research had also been done in the development of vaccines. The important thing to note is that none of the vaccines were being developed for those already infected. The whole point of any vaccine is to create something that could be administered to people to prevent them from being infected by the rest of us. I myself was focused on developing a vaccine that could be administered to babies still inside the womb, so they would be born healthy and free of the virus still devastating the world they would be born into.

You might guess the reason why this aspect was of particular interest to me. I was very pregnant—with twins no less. No particular scientific prowess is needed to do the math and realize that the conception of these two took place the very night that we saw the demise of Forrest Reagan. We were close, very close, to a vaccine that could be administered to babies inside the womb and offer them protection from the viruses that raged outside.

I, too, was running my own kind of race. I was sick. Like everyone else, I had been infected by the virus, but I was lucky, if you could call it that. I was infected with one of the variants that while still deadly, was slow and offered resistance to the other versions. This was certainly not Forrest's intent. He wanted every version to keep the victim susceptible to any other version that came along. I will never know, but I can only hope that it was our own efforts that rushed him to release these bugs that were less than what he wanted.

BUT STILL, I was running a race of my own. I was almost certainly going to die, and unlike most people, I had a pretty good idea of when. My symptoms were relatively minor. A stuffy nose, sore throat, and a fairly persistent cough were almost daily nuisances. I was also inordinately tired and often nauseous, symptoms that could just as easily be explained by pregnancy rather than the virus.

Of course, I wanted to save what remained of the world from the ravages of the virus, but if I were being totally honest, my main goal was to introduce two healthy, virus-free and fertile children into the world. And there was nothing that was going to stop me.

About a month prior, I had done something that would have been unthinkable in my world before the virus. I self-administered a vaccine that would protect my babies from the virus while still in the womb. It was not as crazy or desperate as it might sound. While there had not been any traditional clinical trials, I knew the science was sound. And I was right. At no point had the twins shown any signs of infection, but it was still a race.

The challenge was simple. Could I survive long enough that the twins were viable? Could they survive outside my womb once I was gone? I have never been a particularly religious person, but during any moment that I was not consumed by other thoughts, I prayed to God—not for me, but for the little girl and boy still inside of me.

26

TIGER TELLS THE TALE

Ann was correct, of course. I had never shot anyone before, let alone kill somebody. I had never even raised a weapon with ill intent. In fact, I barely know what I am doing with a gun.

When I first began working with the tribe, I was given exactly three lessons about the care and use of handguns. Those skills had certainly come in handy. It is still surreal to me that I killed somebody. Prior to that day, it was a thought that was unimaginable to me although now, death itself doesn't quite mean the same thing as it did on the day that I killed Forrest.

It is not that life has become cheap. In fact it is quite the contrary. I can't speak for the world, but I can say that I see a world in which life is held all the more dear because we see death all around us every day. Every minute of every day in every corner of the earth is a reminder of the preciousness of life and its fragility.

Even the planet itself seems to be more appreciated than it was before the disaster. In yet another unforeseen consequence of this most horrible crime, people have a different view of this precious little blue ball we all live on. Natural preserves are being established in dozens of nations in hundreds of locations. It seems, at least for now, that seeing the fragility of life has helped us to understand the fragility of our planet.

The tribe had recalled me to Oklahoma two days after the death of Forrest just as the first signs of his crime were becoming clear. Nobody said it outright, but I think they were proud of me, not necessarily for killing Forrest but maybe for making it easier to track the carriers and giving the world a small head start in trying to minimize the damage.

There was a great deal going on among all of the Indigenous American Tribes, but for the moment, they had a very specific assignment for me back in Allset. They wanted me to return to Allset and stay indefinitely for the purpose of recording all of the work being done to treat or cure the viruses. They were already in the process of making their laboratories the focal point of worldwide research.

Converting the laboratories made sense. That's where the virus came from. We had preserved all the data that created the bugs, and we were holding on to the people responsible whether they liked it or not. There would be massive research projects across the globe, but Allset would remain the epicenter.

ON A LARGER SCALE all of the nation's major Indigenous tribes were coming together and organizing for two purposes. First and foremost was to offer as much aid and assistance as possible to any and all research and relief efforts and to everyone affected by the virus.

The other goal was historical. Less than one month after the death of Forrest, my tribe had officially changed our name. For more than a century, we had been called the Nonya, a decision we had no part in making. It was a name that was forced upon us, born of disease, death, and humiliating defeat. None of us alive today have officially known ourselves by any other name.

We had now changed our name back to the Lapannay. Officially, the name is The Lapannay Band of Indigenous Americans. As was explained to me by one of our elders, changing our name was but the first step in reclaiming our heritage and pride. Later, we would begin the work of rebuilding and recording our history. The project would take years and would reconstruct our understanding of our own history going as far back as possible into pre-colonial times.

As I said, that would be for later. For now, the goal was to write a true record of the world tragedy unfolding for all people. All of the Indigenous organizations, but especially the Lapannay, felt strongly that these events should be recorded in truth so future generations could learn from them. I was to be the boots on the ground, recording in real time what happened and what will happen in Allset.

I WAS HONORED and I took this responsibility very seriously. There was no media access to the laboratories in Allset. Hell, there was barely any access to the town at all. The scientists were warned under penalty of law against release of any information. Even the slightest hint would result in the loss of any social media privileges. More serious breaches could result in immediate arrest.

I have wondered to myself why this was of so much importance to my people, but the reasons couldn't be clearer or simpler. We ourselves were the victims of genocide. In many ways, it took place slowly and over centuries, but it was genocide all the same. For those of us who had been called the Nonya, race murder took place almost instantly with smallpox-infected blankets given to them by a man no less sick and twisted than Forrest himself.

Yet the history books have only the most passing reference to this hideous and intentional decimation of our people. Even then, we were painted as savages deserving of these most savage deaths. Our murderers wrote the history books. They hailed themselves as pioneering heroes conquering an untamed continent and bringing to heel the savages who were sometimes in their way.

We are not going to allow the murderers to write the history of this genocide unless you want to count me, the proud killer of the madman who happily killed more than a billion so far and was sure to claim more. In essence, I would be the one to write the history. I, my people, my tribe, and all of Indigenous America would be the ones to write this history, and it would be real.

The heroism of Ann, Ray, and Brian would be known to the world and never forgotten. Records of my own actions, however the world wishes to view them, would be included as well. It is my personal opinion that my own contributions were somewhat exaggerated by my people, but that is, I suppose, understandable and in no way undermines the truth that we now chronicle for the historical record and future generations.

While we were not the main target of this particular genocide, Native American and Inuit deaths were already over a quarter of a million and were sure to climb even higher. Jewish people, who had been victims of a campaign whose goal was also their complete annihilation have suffered horribly again with nearly half a million victims so far, yet they survive and will thrive in this new world just as we will. It is now a connected world, and we will write this terrible history together. Together we will learn from it.

It appears that I myself will survive this disaster but not at all unscathed. The virus has rendered me sterile. I had never decided if I wished to be a father or not. Now there was no choice to be made.

I asked Ann and Ray if I might have the privilege of being declared godfather to their as yet unborn twins. I explained to them that among my people, the role of godfather is more than the simple ceremonial aspect one sees in Western culture. The children would be considered part of the tribe, which was no small thing. No one had ever been made part of our tribe in this way for a century or more. There was no higher honor we could offer. Our elders had extended this invitation, and Ann and Ray had graciously accepted.

Ann and Ray had already decided on names for the twins. They were to be Linda and Brian. They will be given tribal names as well.

It is easy to imagine Linda and Brian as being all of our children, the first to be born in this global village the world is building with their efforts to save our brothers and sisters.

27

THE GOOD DIE YOUNG

I drove my father and Ann home after we returned to Springview that morning. I already knew that my dad was back for good, and I was not at all surprised that Ann, too, would stay. It just seemed natural.

Ann and I went straight to my bedroom. I had kept my own bedroom even after my father had left for Springview, at first because I always suspected he might not care for it there and return at any time. I was right that he might not like the somewhat regimented lifestyle that assisted living facilities provide, even if it meant only regimented mealtimes. Even after he seemed to adapt and enjoy his life there, I just never saw a reason to move into his room. My room was just fine, and now it was fine for both Ann and me.

We went straight to bed with the idea that we get some sleep and then get to work. I was tired but also pretty wired. It's not every day you watch someone get his face blown off. It's pretty shocking even when the face in question richly deserved to be blown off.

It had been a day of firsts: First spy mission, if you could call it that. First murder. First arrest. Amazingly, Ann had almost immediately drifted off to sleep. Looking back now, I think her falling asleep was an act of sheer will and discipline. She knew what was already here. She knew what was coming. And she knew it would take all of her to fight it. She knew she had to sleep, so she slept in the same way an elite athlete might train on a day that they really aren't in the mood to, strictly an act of discipline.

I possess no such discipline and lay next to her watching her sleep for more than an hour. Finally, I rose and walked into the living room. My father sat on the couch, watching the early hours of worldwide terror unfold.

"I knew you would be awake," he said to me. "You're just like me. We're always afraid we're gonna miss something."

"I have a feeling this is something I'd rather miss," I said with the slightest chuckle.

I sat in the recliner next to the couch, and we sat silently for a time, absorbing what we were seeing on the television. I think it was only then that I truly sensed the scope of it all. Up until that moment, everything just kind of happened, one thing after another, and I just acted with that momentum. Now, it really hit me. People were dying. A lot of people will die. I realized I was crying and made no effort to stop.

My father leaned forward on the couch and turned to me. "I am proud of you, son," he said.

That alone roused me enough to begin to halt my tears. I can count on one hand the number of times in my life my father has called me son. I think it was surprise that stopped my tears.

"You may not realize it right now, Ray, but the three of you saved a lot of lives this morning. That fuckface wiped his own computers just an hour or so after you stole the data. If not for the three of you, we would be starting from scratch. Instead, we have a fighting chance.

"Don't get me wrong. It's going to get ugly—very ugly, very

quickly—but always remember, no matter how bad it gets, without the three of you, it would be much worse.

"Listen, since you're awake anyway, you might as well make yourself fuckin' useful. Go back to Springview and get my computer. Bring the paper files too. There won't be a lot. Just grab whatever you see."

That was my father to a T. He would dip a toe into emotional waters and then run in the other direction for fear of getting wet. This was as much as he was ever capable of, and it was enough. Of course, he took no credit for himself.

We could not know it at the time, but literally a billion people or more were estimated to have been saved because of his actions, because he got that device, because he sent us, because he had that guard removed. He never publicly acknowledged those actions, but it didn't matter. Tiger did. Tiger acknowledged them. He recorded for the world everything that was done that night, that morning, and every minute after. Like it or not, Brian Louis (he still never publicly acknowledged the name Litvinov) was a hero, and the world would know it.

I knew better than to try to continue this conversation. He had said what needed to be said, and now the matter was closed. He was moving back home. He needed his computer to keep working at whatever the fuck it was he worked at. I got my shit together and followed his instructions.

The days that followed were a blur of horror and death, but it is still amazing to me how quickly humans can accept the unprecedented as normal and the terrible as routine.

The four of us quickly fell into a rhythm. Every day was basically the same. Ann and I would rise together and go to the lab. My dad would work from the house, and Tiger would always be around. Tiger would help with whatever he was asked, but basically he was just constantly taking notes and pictures with a tablet he carried with him at all times. Everything he collected was sent to the tribal elders, who would share it with leaders of other tribes. Much of the information was also disseminated to social and traditional media as well. They were assembling a real-time history of events.

If I were to be completely truthful, I would have to say that Ann, my dad, and I were never quite comfortable with the role in which we were being cast, but we quickly got used to having Tiger as a friendly shadow. After all, he had every right to be here, and we understood his and the tribe's almost fanatical desire that the truth be known and told.

As for me, I was little more than a do boy. I am no scientist, but I was there with Ann every day, doing whatever was asked of me, whatever was needed. As time passed, what was needed was for me to simply be there and care for Ann.

Of course, it wasn't long before we knew she was sick. It was a given. Everyone was infected, and untold millions were sick and dying. I don't recall Ann talking about being sick even once, but I knew she was and I knew she had symptoms. There was nothing to say. We just went to work.

It wasn't long before we knew she was pregnant as well, but it didn't slow her down. I remember only three times that we left the lab for OB-GYN visits. The first was to confirm that she was indeed pregnant with fraternal twins. The second time was for an ultrasound, and the third was when she actually gave birth. Everything else that was needed to see her through her pregnancy was either already at the lab or brought there by her personal OB-GYN who pretty much set up shop in the lab. The doctor was even given her own office at the lab. Nothing was going to distract Ann from her work.

The work was bearing fruit. The lab at Allset was just one of hundreds brought into operation throughout the world as the virus spread, and the death toll rose, but Allset, with Ann at the helm, set the pace.

. . .

Already there were multiple treatments for multiple versions of the virus. Ann would explain it to me in layman terms as a high stakes game of Whac-A-Mole. Researchers would identify and find a way to tame a particular version of the virus just as another would become more prominent and deadly, but Ann had begun to focus, not surprisingly, on vaccines, not for the living but for prenatal babies and newborns.

Again explaining it to me in layman's terms, there was no point in a vaccine for the infection. Virtually everyone alive was already infected. Some would carry the virus without symptoms. Some would get sick. Many would die. For the living, she would seek treatments. For newborns, she would make it the work of the remainder of her life to find a vaccine.

She and her research team did just that. They developed a prenatal vaccine that appeared to be effective against many strains of the virus. In time, her research would be refined to a point of near perfection, protecting and ensuring the very existence of future generations of Black children and many, many others of varying nationalities.

At that time, it seemed to me like little more than a theory, a promising theory, but still a long way from being a reality. Granted, the distance between theory and reality was shrinking every day as researchers across the globe stood ready to pounce on every potential breakthrough, but even knowing that did not prepare me.

Ann said she was feeling particularly tired that day and wanted to leave early. I was shocked since she never wanted to leave work until the sun went down. Except for that day, I don't remember a single time it was still light outside when we walked into the parking lot.

Tiger was going to join us back at the house. I'm sure he was worried about her health, and I suppose he was also curious about this diversion from our routine. It was unusual, to say the least, but Ann was insistent that Tiger remain at the lab.

"I just want a little alone time with my man," she said just a little too casually.

Tiger is far from stupid, and he totally understood just as I did. There was something she wanted to talk about, now, and privately.

I was driving toward the house when Ann asked, "Why don't we go out for dinner?"

This was also unusual for a lot of reasons. We hadn't had a meal out since this all started. It was mostly delivered dinners and occasional cooking at home with groceries that my dad would go pick up during the day.

"Okay," I answered, "what's your pleasure?"

There weren't a lot of choices of restaurants here in Allset—or anywhere else, for that matter. Massive labor shortages and supply chain disruptions were major effects of the genocide. Many businesses found ways to continue operating, and the economy was slowly adapting to this new normal.

For a time there had been some product shortages and unpredictably large spikes and dips in commodity and stock prices, but for the most part, economic life had not been dangerously disrupted. There had been no widespread food shortages or starvation. Most businesses, including restaurants, were open, maybe not every day or for as many hours, but slowly and surely we were adapting.

"I don't care baby. You pick," she said.

I started toward a place I knew we both like that served Cuban and Mexican food. We ordered delivery from there once every week or two because it was always pretty reliable. We arrived and the lights were on and people were inside, so we knew they were open.

When I went to open the car door, Ann stopped me.

"Ray," she said and paused for a few seconds, "I took the jab."

Those four words shocked me into silence. We had talked about the vaccine for weeks. She had told me that she felt that the prenatal vaccine was ready, and it was the best chance to protect the twins and give them the best chance to be born healthy, but there was a catch. It hadn't been tested yet on anyone, anywhere.

Ann is every bit as cautious and meticulous as any scientist I know, and by this point, I knew a lot of them. In normal times, not a single one of them would ever dream of injecting themselves with an untested, unproven drug of any kind. But these were anything but normal times.

The other problem was the one that shocked me into silence. Ann had told me that the vaccine would almost certainly work, but there was a price— Ann's life. It would shorten her life.

None of us knew how much time she had left, and it was never discussed. The vaccine would protect the children, but further compromise Ann's already weakened immune system. Whereas she might have had months or even years of life remaining, this vaccine all but guaranteed that her expected lifespan might be measured only in weeks, maybe days. She was sacrificing her own life for the twins. It really was that simple. It was why in that moment I could only feel anger and confusion.

"I thought that was a decision we were going to make together," I said. "I should have had some say in this . . . some choice."

"No, honey," she said, "because you could never have made the right choice, nor could I have ever expected you to. I couldn't let you live a life of guilt and regret. This could only be my choice, and I promise you, my love, it was not made lightly. I love you. I love my life, but I also know that by taking this vaccine, I can protect our babies and so many others. What does a few extra months or years mean compared to that?"

I held her gaze with eyes filled with pain. "They mean everything because we would have spent them together," I said.

She reached for my hand and pulled it to her lips. "I know, my love, and I am so sorry. You are the love of my life, and I have cherished every moment with you, and now you will be the one to raise these healthy beautiful babies . . . well, you and that grumpy old bastard back at the house." Her mouth curled into a sly smile.

As much as it hurt, I would later tell Tiger many of the details of this moment. The world should know. They should know of her brilliance, her bravery, and her selfless sacrifice for her children and all the world's children.

"When?" I asked, and she knew exactly what I was talking about.

The babies would be delivered by C-section, and I knew this woman well enough to know that she had already planned that as well.

"In three days," she said. "I will be just short of thirty-eight weeks at that point, and that will be the ideal time. Every day we wait puts them at risk."

This was now Ann the scientist speaking, and there was no point in arguing. Today was Tuesday. Thursday evening she would be admitted into the hospital. Friday morning, if all went well, I would be a father.

"I can't go in there," I said. "Let's go home."

I started the car and drove in silence for the less than ten-minute trip. I honestly can't recall what I was feeling during those minutes. There was just too much, too fast, and I couldn't even begin to process it. I only knew that I loved this woman, now more than ever, and I was doomed to lose her. Whereas that used to be a theory, like everything else, it had quickly become a reality.

When we walked into the house, there was my father seated at a desk in front of his computer.

"How was dinner?" he asked with a smile, but his tone quickly changed when he saw the look on my face.

"You told him?" he asked, already knowing the answer.

That was it. That was enough for me to break.

"You knew?" I yelled angrily at my father. "Of course you fuckin' knew! You know everything, don't you? All the time, you know everything!"

It was Ann who answered. "It's not his fault, Ray. It was my decision, mine alone, and I told him first only so he could have everything in place at the hospital . . . simple logistics."

I looked at them both, shaking my head.

"The two of you . . . you are fuckin' robots."

Even as I said it, I knew it wasn't true. I knew full well the emotional toll on both of them. Ann was no Brian. She was not afraid of her feelings, and she embraced them. But she was also a scientist, a logical, ordered scientist. For her, what was being done made sense. It was the right thing to do.

I retreated into the bedroom with Ann following close behind. We sat next to each other on the bed. I saw the fullness of her belly, and for the first time, I could see the weariness in her face. She was still beautiful, but she was tired. It truly was a race, one she was determined to win.

In that moment, my anger faded, and all that was left was love. We embraced. We kissed. We made love one final time, made all the sweeter by the caution and pace that was the only possible way.

I don't remember if we ever got around to eating anything that night. I only remember how peacefully she slept, how at peace she was with her decision.

It was selfish of me to have my doubts, but I believe I have that right. I have earned that much. I held no further anger toward my father or Ann, for that matter. The three of us simply woke up the next morning and went back to work that day . . . and the next.

My father had indeed planned the logistics, and Ann was admitted into a private room with little fanfare at something close to midnight. We weren't exactly hiding. It was certainly no secret that Ann was pregnant, but by this point, we were full-blown celebrities, and we needed as much peace and calm as possible. As usual, Brian Louis delivered.

And so did Ann. At 6:30 a.m. the next morning, Tiger, my father, and I watched through a window as Brian and Linda entered the world via Caesarean section. I was allowed in immediately following the birth. Ann and I held each child in turn for a precious few minutes until they were whisked away to incubators that had already been set up in her room.

I had one minute alone with Ann before she was taken away to post-op. Tiger had been permitted a single photo to be taken through the window. He actually took several to make sure he had at least one good one but as promised, he used only one.

The birth had gone exactly to plan, and we had two healthy, virus-free babies, and they would remain virus free. They were the first children born in that condition in this post genocide world. If forced to describe them in these terms I would say they were beautiful "Black" babies, Linda sharing the skin tone and beauty of her mother, Brian, more light-skinned and sharing some of my own facial features but still, thankfully, looking very much like his mother.

It was supposed to have been only a few minutes until Ann would be returned to her room, but the heart abnormality had shown up almost immediately after she had given birth. It was almost two agonizing hours before she was returned to her room, fast asleep.

I think we already knew, but the doctor quickly confirmed our worst fears. The virus had damaged Ann's heart—as it was designed to do. The vaccine, the stress of pregnancy, and giving birth had all taken their toll.

I have noticed that doctors understandably do not like to say that someone is going to die, so the way the doctor explained it to us was that Ann was unlikely to ever leave the hospital. I hope it made her feel better to say it like that. It did no such thing for us.

We watched the babies sleep. We watched Ann sleep. Tiger took no pictures, made no notes. My father made no comments save for the astonishing beauty of his grandchildren. With that I could not disagree.

Ann finally awoke in the late afternoon. It was a rather hectic room with doctors and nurses coming and going, caring for the babies and Ann. The incubators had been strictly precautionary, and technically neither baby required one. We were able to hold them.

Ann could not stand, but she was able to hold her babies, and she did, even holding both at once for a short time. As evening came, my father and Tiger both went home, my father back to the house and Tiger back to The Hope where he was still staying.

I, of course, was staying with Ann in the room, and our small family finally had a little bit of alone time. Ann and the babies mostly sleeping. I was wide awake throughout. By about 7 a.m. I did finally fall asleep and awoke about 10 a.m. to the sound of Ann's heart monitor. It would ring an alarm from time to time, reflecting the instability of Ann's heart and vital signs. This time was no worse than any other, but it was enough to wake me from my short sleep. Ann was awake and somewhat upright in the bed, holding Linda. Brian was quietly dreaming in the incubator.

Later, I spotted a Rabbi in the hospital corridor. Our eyes met briefly. I realized that he recognized me. I had an idea. I asked the Rabbi if he was going to be in the hospital for a while and he said yes.

"Great," I said hurriedly. "I'll be right back."

I raced back to the room and seeing Ann awake, I announced in a way that I thought was quite grand, "Let's get married!"

Her response was not quite what I expected.

"You mean now? Like right now?" she asked while I just kind of nodded my head and grinned enthusiastically.

"Yes, of course, Ray. This is the wedding every little girl dreams of... in a hospital, attached to 57 wires and looking like shit."

I was undeterred.

"Yes," I said, "that sucks, but marry me. Now!"

Our eyes met. She smiled.

"Oh, for fuck's sake, Ray. Yes, of course I will marry you."

"Great," I said. "I'll be right back."

I ran back down the corridor and passed by my dad and Tiger who were returning for a visit.

"I'll be right back," I yelled again as I passed.

I found the Rabbi and realized for the first time from his clothing that this was clearly a devout, orthodox Rabbi.

"Do you perform weddings?" I asked quickly. Maybe saying hello first would have been better.

He was a bit taken by surprise but recovered quickly and said, "Yes, of course. Are you Jewish?"

"Well, yes, uh, no, well, sort of. It's kind of difficult to explain . . . Does it matter?"

From the look on his face, I got the sense that it very much mattered. He paused for a few seconds, clearly considering it before answering.

"No, it doesn't. Where is the lucky bride?"

And so we were married, in the eyes of God anyway. We would need a license if we wanted the State of New York to come on board. I think the Rabbi was a bit star-struck and tongue-tied when he realized that it was indeed Tiger, Brian, Ann and me. I realized then what a good job Tiger had really done.

Tiger and my dad had been a bit surprised when I appeared at the door with what was clearly a very devout, Hassidic Rabbi. I called them both my best man. Linda served as the maid of honor. No, it was not the dream wedding every little girl dreams of, but it was beautiful. Ann was beautiful. And despite her scolding, I knew she was happy.

My father disappeared for a little while and then reappeared. He had gone home and come back. He reached in his pocket and pulled out a ring.

"It's not a proper wedding day without a ring," he said tentatively and held out the ring for Ann. "This was Ray's mother's ring," he said. "I want you to have it . . . if it's not too weird."

He looked over at me and then back to Ann.

"No, Brian," Ann said. "It's not too weird. It's beautiful. Thank you."

I scurried over and helped Ann put the ring on. It fit. a little loosely, but it fit.

We enjoyed a day of relative calm. There was no discussion of the future, just an appreciation of the now, just the beauty of the children. The nervousness of the Rabbi and my own impulsive wedding planning were the source of laughter and joy. Tiger and my dad stayed well into the evening but eventually went home and again left us with what we all knew was precious time. I could see in Ann's face that there was something she wanted to talk about. I had learned the signs.

"I want you to call your friend, Lee," she said seemingly out of nowhere, but I knew better.

We had no secrets. Ann knew about my prior relationship

with Lee back in Las Vegas, and she knew we were still friends. We would speak on the phone every week or two and keep up to date on social media.

"Call Lee and ask her if she would come here to Allset and help you with the babies. You know you are going to need help."

To be honest, part of me was feeling very manipulated. Was this the love of my life telling me to get back together with my old girlfriend after she is gone?

She sensed my discomfort and said, "No, Ray, I'm not trying to tell you what to feel. Just bring her here if she'll come. These children will need a mother's love. Maybe she can fill that role, and maybe she can't, but at least they will have someone who is emotionally open. You've come a long way, but that's not you, and it sure as shit isn't your dad. So just have her come and stay . . . if she will . . . See how it plays out."

Nothing more was said on the matter. I wasn't even that surprised. This was Ann, the strength, the single mindedness, and yes, the practicality.

SHE DIED in my arms the next morning. There had been some talk of emergency surgery, even a heart transplant, but it was never really a consideration. Ann knew the odds of her survival were virtually nonexistent. My last sight of her was in her bed, her hard-fought-for children nearby, healthy and strong.

The funeral and the days after are a blur. It is amazing what the human mind can do to protect itself. I remember little or nothing of the funeral and the days after. Tiger chronicled the events tastefully, and it was all there for me to see if I ever wished to.

The next week, the town of Allset officially changed its name again. It will forever be known as Byronville in honor of the scientist and my wife, who was born Ann Byron. It was known that we had married, and I had been asked if Byronville would be okay with me. It was. After all, there was already a Louisville, and I don't think anyone would want to come to Litvinovtown or anything like that. At least this time, they spelled it right, and I'd like to think that the town elders of over a century ago would be very well satisfied. There was no Edison, but Byronville would be on the cutting edge of science for the foreseeable future.

28

SWIMMING WITH BABY SHARKS

It is three years later, and we are at my house, well, mine and Ray's anyway. The poker game of the day is in full swing. Sitting around our table are Ray, Slick, Alex, Sid, Lenny, Tiger, and I. Tiger, believe or not, had become a respectable player, unlike our other two guests that Ray had invited from The Hope, who had been selected based on having deep pockets and an astonishing lack of poker skill.

A now three-year-old Linda sits in my lap watching my every move. Little Brian is standing near Ray but moves closer to me as he sees Slick push in a big pile of chips and declare, "All in."

I'm the only other player left in the hand. Do I call his big bet, or do I fold my hand and give Slick the huge pot? I didn't have much of a hand myself, but I did have a pair, and I could beat any outright bluff. If Slick held nothing and was bluffing, I would win by calling. If he held any kind of decent hand, I would lose—and lose big. It was a big pot. It was a big bet.

"What do you think, Tooby?" I asked my three-year-old namesake Brian.

He had become "Tooby" because we had started calling him

"Two-B," kind of like Brian the second. It had somehow morphed into Tooby, and he seemed to like it, so it stuck.

Tooby eyed my hand, looked at the five board cards, and then squinted across the table at Slick in a sort of three-year-old version of a stare down. He was looking, as was I, for any sign of weakness from Slick, but before he could say anything, Linda blurted out, "He's got poopy, Grandpa. You should call."

Slick reacted instantly. "Oh, what the fuck! How many Litvinovs do I have to play against?"

He was right, of course. Even Tiger called me out.

"Hey, Brian," he said, "I saw somebody walking by on the street. Should we ask them if you should call?"

Poker is an individual game and showing my hole cards and asking for help would have gotten me thrown out of any casino in the world, but on the other hand, they are three. They wouldn't have been at any casino in the first place.

"Okay," I said. "I call."

The moment I said it, Slick surrendered, throwing his hand face down toward the dealer. The entire table, including Slick, erupted in laughter. Slick had been bluffing. Tooby and Lin helped me stack up the chips that used to be Slick's.

Lee walks in from the kitchen, takeout menu in hand. "Anybody hungry?" she asks. "I'm going to order Chinese."

Hands go up. Orders are blurted out. Well, at least here I won't be late for dinner.

The game stops for a few minutes as everybody shouts out their orders. I call Tiger over for a moment. I hold three pieces of paper in my hand. The first two are the checks given to me by Forrest. I had never cashed them.

"Here," I said as I handed him the checks. "These should probably be part of the historical record."

"You could have cashed them first, you know," Tiger replied, folding the two checks and putting them in his pocket. "What's this?" he asks as I hand him the other piece of paper.

I said, "You will know what to do with it" as explanation. On that page was the only public statement I ever made, and he did know what to do with it.

The almost inconceivable horror that we have all witnessed appears to be over . . . for now.

The world's answer to this crisis has been so collectively magnificent as to seem the stuff of fiction, almost like a movie where mankind comes together to fight an alien invasion. But this was no alien. It was one of us using only the tools that we ourselves created.

I am told that our actions saved many lives, that we are heroes. It doesn't feel that way, nor should it. Like all of us, I failed to stop a horrible crime, the most horrible crime ever by and against humanity.

So now what? Now we must all be heroes. There is no other way. The tools of death still surround us. These weapons still exist and people will still be people. We must grow or die. It is that simple. We must continue to grow beyond our childish greed and hate.

There is reason for hope. We have seen great nations rise above centuries of hostility to save lives. Perhaps each of us can do the same. Nothing less will do. We must be better.

I would truly be a hero if I could promise you this will not ever happen again, but I cannot. We must all continue to grow. We must all *be heroes. There is no other way we can survive.*

I wish us luck.

Brian Louis

AUTHOR'S NOTES

How do I write a story where more than one billion people die in a horrible way?

How could it ever seem anything but glib and dismissive in the face of the scale of the tragedy within these pages?

How is it possible to honor and respect the impact of the loss of even a single individual in the face of death on such a massive scale?

I don't know if it is even possible. But I tried to detail the scale and horror of these events while not subjecting the reader to relentless and constant despair. Again, I do not know if I was successful. Nor do I know if it is even possible.

What I tried to do was create real people who are affected by these horrible events and yet retain their humanity despite it.

They are not super-human. They are scared and flawed humans in a terrifying world that is becoming worse with every passing moment.

They each accomplish some remarkable things but not in any super-heroic way. They are just people. Good people doing their best as the world burns around them.

It is my hope that you, dear reader, can find something of yourself in one or more of them. Because there is nothing they do that we ourselves cannot do.

But should you also find yourself in some sympathy with the devil, please do not despair. It means only that there is still work to be done. This we already know.

The choice, as always, is yours.

ABOUT THE AUTHOR

David Litvin has spent most of his adult life in two worlds. The first was in the Basque sport of Jai Alai. He was the U.S National Amateur Jai-Alai champion in 1990. He played jai alai in the Campeonato De Mundial (World Championship) in Havana, Cuba, as part of the Pan American Games. As a representative of the United States, a fourth-place finish earned the U.S. a berth in the 1992 Olympic Games in Barcelona, Spain. Later, his attention turned to the world of poker where he was a profitable, professional player and later a poker dealer, poker tournament director, and poker room director.

His previous work is a musical stage play about the world of high stakes poker, *All In: The Poker Musical,* which featured original songs by Grammy award winner Vini Poncia.

He tries to keep his needs simple and his masters few.

THE AUTHOR MAY BE REACHED AT:
DLKOSMO@GMAIL.COM OR
DAVIDLITVIN.COM

ALSO BY DAVID L. LITVIN

Frum God: The Mostly True Adventures of a Modern Day Messiah

All In: The Poker Musical

Silencer's End

Why the Fuck Not?

Milton Keynes UK
Ingram Content Group UK Ltd.
UKHW022114290224
438689UK00013BA/643